THE DEATH OF JACKY JOHNSTONE

Written by Edward Gowdy

Published in 2018 by Edward Gowdy

This book is a work of fiction. Any names, characters,
places or situations are a product of the author's imagination
or used fictitiously. Any resemblance to actual
people (living or dead), locations or events is coincidental.

This book is in no way affiliated with, endorsed by, or
associated with the brands or companies mentioned in the book.
They have been used purely for the purposes of the story.

Dedicated to my mother, Maureen, and all the people
who made me laugh and smile, who are now gone.
That laughter had to be paid for in tears.

CHAPTER ONE
BEDSIDE MEMORIES

You would be forgiven for thinking that people only died in hospital at night. Loved ones standing in brightly-lit, sterilised corridors. Lonely, heartbroken and having no sense of anything around them. The truth is, people die in hospital during the morning, the evening, the afternoon and at night. There is no set time or convenient time to die. The cattle-like hustle and bustle of a hospital in daylight hours hides all the pain and tears of the grief-stricken. Does anyone really care anyway? Does anyone really give too much thought to a stranger whose life will never be the same? The simple answer is: they don't. I'll guarantee you that they care more about where they are parked than a stranger's life being devastated forever.

There were an estimated 3,600 people killed in the so-called Irish 'troubles'. I'll not dissect them into categories – British soldiers, RUC, Catholics, Protestants – because it doesn't matter. Once we start categorising those who died, they become statistics. It's a callous practice; one that serves no purpose other than to play the blame game, or for one section to shift guilt from themselves to another, or historians trying to analyse for the sake of preventing it happening again, but it always does. Try telling the families or closest friends that their loved one was number 100, or 300, or 3,000. It would mean nothing. The point I'm trying to make is, although Jacky Johnstone wasn't a victim of the troubles, he falls into the category of every other death. In my opinion, nobody really cares except the immediate family. I myself stand guilty of this. I'm not ashamed of it because I know I'm no different to anybody else. My mother and a good friend were the closest people I know to have passed and, although there have been many others I have known who have passed away, I can state that their deaths had no effect on me in any way.

When does a death start to become truly painful? The most painful? I doubt anyone would disagree with me when I say it's when a mother loses a child. A mother will always look on the person they brought into the world as their 'child'. Whether they are a new born or a fifty-year-old, it's her 'child'.

May Johnstone stood in one of those brightly-lit, sterilised corridors we only find in hospitals. She stood outside a room sobbing. Inside the room was her boy. Her boy's spirit had passed from his body to wherever he believed his spirit would pass. He was dead.

"There was nothing more we could do for him, Mrs Johnstone," said the emotionless doctor, wearing baggy eyes and a slight growth.

"Can I have a few minutes with him before you take him away, doctor?"

"Of course you can. Take as long as you like." With that, the doctor scampered away to get himself a sandwich and maybe a couple of hours sleep before his next fourteen-hour shift.

May stood outside the closed door. Behind the door lay the lifeless body of her boy. Her only child. She entered the room. Turning the oversized lever on the door was one of the hardest things May had ever done in her seventy years on Earth.

As she stepped inside, she was shaking. She looked at her motionless child on the bed. What she saw – or what she thought she saw, at first – horrified her, and it wasn't the limp carcass of her forty-year-old child. The first thing she noticed was his baldness. It's funny how the mind works. In such a horrendous moment, all she could think about was her son's silly vanity. I might call it silly but, to her and her son, it could have been the most important thing in the world. Everything's relative. Only Jacky and his mother knew he was bald. Through all his problems, he kept it a secret. May wasn't going to let him down now. She rushed back into the corridor, guarding the door from the outside so no one could enter the room and see her bald son. She drew the attention of a nurse who was passing.

"Nurse, nurse, can I have a word?"

"Yes, love, can I help you?"

"My son, Jacky." May pointed to the closed door.

"Yes, what about him?" said the nurse, looking at the closed door.

"Where's his hair?"

The nurse looked a little inquisitively at May, thinking for a split second that she had bumped into someone from the psychiatric ward.

"His hair? What do you mean?" she asked May politely. The nurse had had plenty of dealings with the old and infirm. She knew not to take things they say too seriously.

"It's not on his head. It's gone."

"I don't know where it is, love. Had he chemotherapy?"

"No, he hadn't had chemotherapy. It must have been on his head earlier when he came in."

"Why don't you ask him?" replied the nurse, not having the slightest idea what May was talking about.

May looked at the nurse. The nurse had no idea her baby boy was dead, and she certainly had no idea where his toupee was. She walked away from the nurse without uttering another word. Walking back into the room where Jacky was lying, May closed the door behind her. As the door closed, May could hear the nurse shouting to a colleague that if they didn't hurry the canteen would be closed. May wasn't upset that the nurse didn't know her son was dead. She wasn't

5

even fully aware of Jacky's death. At this moment in time, she was only concerned about the nakedness of Jacky's head. She was letting her son down by letting him lie here, for all the world to see. Bald.

She wished now that she hadn't phoned Ted. He would be on his way. Maybe she should phone him back and say they had already taken Jacky away? She couldn't. She never lied. What a silly old woman, she thought. Her son's dead and all she can worry about is a silly old toupee. May wondered, now that Jacky was gone, was it that important? Should she not be concerned with more important things? After all, she didn't mind that he was bald. No, she must find it. May checked the little bedside drawers and cabinets, then she checked the toilet and under his pillow. It wasn't there.

She sat down on the chair beside Jacky for a breather – just for a breather – then she planned to look again. She had just sat down when she spied out of the corner of her eye something lying in the corner behind the door. At first, it looked like a dead rat, but then she realised what it was. How did it get there? Did it fall off as they wheeled him in? Were the doctors throwing it at each other for a laugh? Doctors don't do such things, she assured herself. Maybe orderlies? Maybe the orderlies were playing with it, mocking Jacky, mocking her son. No matter, she thought. She lifted it and placed it on Jacky's head. There now. That's better. She was now able to start the grieving process.

May sat beside the lifeless body of her son. She held his hand, her finger tips caressing the back of his. His hands aren't that cold, she thought to herself. They were colder when he used to bring in the scuttles of coal from the backyard on winter nights. They were colder when he used to clear her path of snow over the years. Even colder than when he was a young boy, coming back in the door after playing out with his friends. She was sure they were far colder the night she found him outside the homeless shelter. Why did he do that? There was always a home for him at her house, the family home. He didn't need to go anywhere else. Her Jacky never wanted to be a burden, but he was never a burden to May. Belfast was a cold place in the winter, she thought. But then so is anywhere if you have no money for heating. Jacky used to crawl into bed beside her until he was a brave age. May thought of how alone Jacky would be now in the graveyard. Her boy all alone. It never dawned on her how alone *she* would be now, what with Jacky senior dead, too. But this was May – a lady who never gave a thought about herself.

She sat stroking his hand. She remembered when they put him in gaol. The story still made her smile.

Jacky was off the drink for a couple of weeks. He did this occasionally, a scare off the doctor maybe, or saving up for a special occasion. Of course, saving for a special occasion meant that he saved his drinking money for a couple of weeks so he could drink it all in one day – at a wedding or birthday party or something of the like.

Nevertheless, when he wasn't drinking, he had a wee flutter on the horses. The working-class people in Belfast are no different than those in Manchester, Liverpool or Yorkshire. They either drink or gamble, but the majority do both. On this particular day, Jacky had a twenty pence Yankee. For those not familiar with the ins and outs of the joys of horse-backing, a twenty pence Yankee costs two pounds twenty. You pick four horses. If four win, you would usually win big. If three win, your winnings would be slashed. If two win, you'll be lucky to get your money back. Jacky, this day, had three winners and one beat. Jacky counted forty-eight pounds of the bet – not a bad day's work, he'd thought, as he strolled cheerfully to the betting shop to collect his winnings.

Betting shops were drab, monotonous places in those days. For years there were no front windows allowed. I'm sure the government meant well with this policy, probably brought this law in so that children couldn't see their fathers' wasting ways and, therefore, would hopefully not follow suit. It suited the gambling man though. That scourge of every punter – the wife – couldn't see her husband gambling his life away as she passed the bookies in the street.

They were smoked-filled in those days. People shouting at the TV screen as if the shouts would make the horses go faster. Cursing and throwing beaten dockets on the floor. Pat Eddery, a top jockey, would be a *wanker* and *couldn't ride his wife* one day if he was on a horse that beat your bet. The next day, if you had him on a winner, he would be *the best jockey alive*. In Belfast, they also had a doorman in the bookmakers – usually an elderly man who let you in. You buzzed the buzzer, he opened the door for you. This old fellow would probably spend all day in the place anyway if he didn't work there, so why not get paid for it? He was there because of the threat of an opposing faction coming in and spraying the place with bullets, not because of any hatred for punters, but because there were always so many people confined to a small place that the bullets would cause maximum carnage. It didn't stop anyone going to the bookmakers. It did, however, make every man turn and look every time the door opened.

Jacky got buzzed in. He was on good form. He thanked John for letting him in. John, the doorman, acknowledged his gratitude with a nod. Jacky proceeded to the counter. There were four windows at the counter, each with a clerk. There were three windows for placing a bet, one window for paying out winning bets. You would think that people would have caught onto this – three to place a bet and one to pay out – but they didn't. Jacky placed his winning docket on the pay-out counter and slid it under the window. The clerk handed Jacky twenty-two pounds.

"There's forty-eight pounds of that bet, mate," Jacky said to the clerk, thinking he had made a genuine mistake, and would do a quick recount and hand over the rightful amount.

"There's twenty-two pounds of it. Now could you move away from the counter? There's another customer behind you," responded the clerk, used to unsavoury antics from punters.

"How do you make that out?" asked Jacky, a little sterner.

"Because I can fucking count, that's why."

Jacky was furious at the clerk's customer service. He was getting angry. He held up two fingers. "Can you count these?"

"What are you talking about?" asked the clerk, looking at the two fingers Jacky had placed in front of his eyes.

"Can you count how many fingers are going to rip your eyeballs out if you don't pay me my money?"

The clerk started to get nervous and tried to calm the situation. "Look, Jacky, you had two winners and two beat, there's twenty-two pounds of the bet."

Jacky pointed to the betting docket that was sitting behind the glass. "Look, *three* winners, Big Ben, Gold digger and Red Kite. *Three* winners."

The clerk lifted the docket and pointed to one of the horses written down. "Red Kite didn't win," he informed Jacky.

"What did you mean, it didn't win? It won the last race on TV," replied Jacky, now positive it was an error on the clerk's behalf.

"Red *Kit* won the last race on TV. Not Red *Kite*." The clerk was looking a little smug now.

Jacky was getting angry again. "So, what? I misspelt it. It was a TV Yankee, you know rightly what I meant."

"There was a greyhound out called Red Kite today. It was beaten. That's the name you had on your bet slip and that's the name I'm going to settle the bet on. Your mistake, not mine. I only work here, I don't make the rules."

Jacky stared at the clerk. The old 'rules are rules, I only work here' chestnut. The words used by people who shaft other people then blame it on other people. Jacky knew the score. He could stand here all day and argue with this clown behind the counter and he still wouldn't get the twenty-six quid of which he was robbed. Next it would be 'my hands are tied' or 'do you want me to get the sack?' – Jacky had heard it all before. Jacky lifted the twenty-two pounds and quietly walked out of the bookies. He didn't utter another word.

Jacky knew exactly what he was going to do when he left the betting shop. He had heard people in these situations before when they get hard done by. They would threaten to kill this and that, lose their money elsewhere, wreck the place, burn the place to the ground... but no one ever did. Not Jacky – he wasn't going to say it but not follow through with his threats. He *was* going to burn the place down.

That night, Jacky acquired some petrol. To this day, May doesn't know where he got the petrol from. She knew where he got the balaclava from. She bought it for him, for cold winter days at work. Jacky was calm as he walked to the place that had robbed him earlier. All he could think of was that he had twenty-two pounds in his pocket and he should have forty-eight. 'Rules are rules' he remembered the clerk saying. Well *fuck him,* he thought to himself. The rules are, there are no rules. That's the rules of the jungle. He then thought to himself about the pile of shite he was thinking – *rules of the jungle.* He got a little embarrassed at his thoughts, but not embarrassed in the slightest about walking down the street with a can of petrol and a balaclava in his pocket.

As Jacky stepped into the doorway of the bookies, he pulled the balaclava over his head. He had an urge to pour the petrol through the letter box, throw a match in, and run. Of course, it didn't work out like that. As he entered the doorway, he tripped on something.

"What the fuck? I'm trying to get some kip here."

He had stepped on a homeless man trying to get a night's slumber in the doorway.

"What are you doing here?" Jacky asked, startled, taking off his balaclava.

"What are *you* doing here? What's that in your hand?" asked the homeless man, pointing at the petrol.

"Never mind what it is. You're going to have to move on."

"Move on? Where? Do you know how hard it is to get a spot? Is that petrol? Any chance of a sniff?"

"No, you can't have a sniff. You're going to have to move on. There's an operation going on here."

"An operation? What operation? IRA?"

"No."

"UVF?"

"No!"

"Then who? Who's the operation for?"

"Never mind. You'll just have to move on, I don't want you getting hurt."

"Listen, mate, do your operation, do whatever you have to do. I don't care. I'm going nowhere."

"Just fuck off. I don't want you getting burned."

"No."

"So, you don't care if you get burned alive then?"

"I don't want to get burned alive but I'll take my chances before I lose this spot."

"You're going to lose it anyway once I burn this place to a cinder. Have you nowhere else to go?"

"There's a wee bed and breakfast around the corner."

"Then go there."

"I can't."

"Why?"

"What a silly question! Do you think if I'd any money for a bed and breakfast I'd be sleeping here?"

"How much is it?"

"Twenty-five pounds a night."

"That's cheap."

"I know. And they do a good breakfast."

Jacky looked down at the homeless man. He reached into his pocket, finding the twenty-two pounds he had collected from the bet earlier. He took out the money and handed it to the homeless guy.

The homeless guy took the money, counted it, and was a little displeased. "There's only twenty-two pound here."

"It's all I have."

"Well it's not enough. They won't give me a room if I'm three pounds short."

"They probably wouldn't give you a room anyway – not for a hundred pounds – you smell like shit."

"There's no call for that. You try being homeless, see how you smell."

"Look, do you want the twenty-two quid to fuck off or will I take it back off you?"

"OK, OK, I'll take it, but there's no need for the insults."

The homeless guy walked away muttering and moaning about being rudely awakened and how he needed another three pounds for the bed and breakfast. It wasn't long before he was out of sight.

Jacky poured the petrol through the letterbox and tossed in a lit match. It was that easy. The flames climbed up the door and soon had engulfed the building. Not that Jacky saw any of it – he was away as soon as he threw in the match.

There was around sixty thousand pounds' worth of damage done to the betting shop – all because he was paid twenty-six pounds short on his bet. He had given the homeless guy twenty-two pounds. This left him with nothing. He ended up with not a penny of his bet that was totally legit. Jacky was shortly arrested for the arson, charged and got six months in gaol. The homeless man gave evidence against him to get off a shoplifting charge. May went to every court appearance and visited Jacky every week.

May liked this story about Jacky. She liked the way he was kind to the homeless man. He made him leave so as not to get burnt, and gave him money.

Heart of gold, Jacky. It never crossed her mind what kind of person would be capable of burning a building for the sake of twenty-six pounds. To May, that was irrelevant. She could only see the good in him.

May sat alone, caressing her son's hand. She spoke softly to him.

"I hope you put on that clean underwear I brought you up. You'll be seeing big Jacky up there. He'll look after you."

The door opened. It was Ted. He walked straight over to May, put an arm around her and kissed her on the head.

"Are you OK, love?" He half whispered into her ear.

"I'm OK, Ted. Thanks for coming, I hope you weren't doing anything important."

"When do the likes of us do anything important, May? Anyway, what could be more important than this?"

Ted and May were very close. They were the last of a dying breed. Old school. Ted had gotten Jacky a start on the building sites more than once. May would ask Ted as a favour when Jacky wasn't working. Ted knew Jacky was an alcoholic and alcoholics would always let you down. Ted got Jacky starts because May asked. If May knew how much Ted was sticking his neck out by getting Jacky started, she would never have asked. Ted would get him a start, and it always ended up the same. Jacky wouldn't weigh in some mornings.

"*Where's Jacky?*" the boss would ask.

"I don't know, I don't live with him," Ted would reply.

Ted knew it was senseless making excuses for alcoholics. If he made one excuse, he would be making them forever.

Ted went through Jacky one time. A work colleague told him that Jacky had brought a couple of beers in, for a cure. He may have gone through Jacky but he went through the guy that told him even harder for telling tales. That was Ted. Old school.

"He was only a young man. What's it all about, Ted?" asked May as Ted pulled up a chair beside her.

"I don't know, May, I just don't know. It must be inner city Belfast, inner city anywhere, they all seemed to be caught up in a drink culture."

"All of them, Ted? All the young people these days?"

"Well, not all of them, May. Some escape it; the lucky ones."

"Do you think it was self-inflicted, Ted? Do you think if you drink yourself to death, it's like suicide?"

"May, don't concern yourself with ifs and buts. Your big lad's gone and no ifs, buts or whys are ever going to bring him back. You need to start thinking about yourself now. I'm here if you need me, you know that."

"I know you are, Ted, thank you."

"No thanks required, May, I'm here for whatever you need."

"You know, Ted, I always thought I would lead the way. When I started my young family all those years ago, I hoped I would be the first to die. I somehow thought that, after death, I would be able to let the two Jackys know that it wasn't that bad; when you die, everything will be all right. What a silly old woman I am. Do you think he's in a better place, Ted?"

"Of course he is, May. He's with big Jack now. He'll look after him."

Ted, although he never put much thought into the afterlife, knew this is what May wanted to hear, and keeping May happy was his only concern right now.

They sat silent for a while, May with her thoughts, Ted with his. The silence didn't last long though. It was broken by a quiet tap on the door, which then opened and a head appeared from behind it.

It was an ugly head. A thin-faced, chiselled-chinned ugly head. Bald at the front, long, grey hairs at the back. An unlikable face. A gaunt, hooked-nosed unlikable face. He wasn't invited into the room but he stepped into it anyway. He wore a black jacket, grey, pinstriped trousers and a shirt that was grey but had once been white. He was like something that had just walked off the set of a 1920s black and white horror movie. It was Bartholomew Butt, the undertaker. Speaking in a broad Irish accent – let's say, traveller's brogue – he turned his attention to May.

"Mrs Johnstone, how are you, my dear?"

Bartholomew put both his hands out, expecting May to stand up and hug him. May stayed seated, as did Ted, just staring at the thing in front of them. Bartholomew realised no such embrace was coming, so he quickly dropped his hands. He looked down at Jacky, and continued.

"Ah, poor Jacky, what a waste of a young life, plucked in his prime. What was he? Thirty-one? Thirty-two?"

Both May and Ted stared in disbelief. Both stayed silent, not knowing exactly what was in front of them or what it was doing there. He ignored their silence and continued as if he had known these people his whole life.

"It's only because the big man upstairs wants him all to himself. Isn't that right, Mr Johnstone? I take it you'll be having a good send off for him then."

At that, Bartholomew kissed his forefingers and placed them on Jacky's face, something that May hadn't yet had the chance to do. Ted, thinking at first that this man may have known May, soon realised after being called Mr Johnstone that neither himself nor May had ever met this person before, but he had an idea who the man was, and Ted had heard enough.

"Are you having a laugh?" Ted asked, in a manner that suggested he knew the answer.

The undertaker looked surprised at Ted's tone. "I'm sorry, Mr Johnstone? Is there a problem?"

"Don't pretend you know me. You don't know me. I'm not Mr Johnstone. The only Mr Johnstone in this room is the one in the box. Are you in here trying to sell this woman a coffin before her child's even cold?"

"I am trying to sell nothing, sir. I come in times of need, to release the burden of the burial and all it entails unto me. I provide a service. A service in which I give the grief-stricken one less thing to worry about in their darkest hour."

"So, you're here to hand out free coffins and free burials?"

"They're not free, sir, and I find it a little discourteous that money should be brought up, when this young man lies tragically deceased before us, before his very soul has even left the room."

Ted was angry. "Before his soul has left the room? You were probably standing outside before he'd even died."

"I was not."

"How did you know this boy was dead? Do you pay off a porter to ring you every time a patient has died or near death? A nurse? A receptionist? Or have you been monitoring his progress with his local GP?"

"I do no such things, sir. It's a calling."

"It's a calling, is it? I know what I'm calling you. Bartholomew, isn't it?"

"It is. Bartholomew Butt. The most respected funeral director in the city."

"I knew it! I've heard of you. You're Bart the Bastard."

"That is not me, sir. It's someone else you're thinking of. I'm held in the highest esteem."

"Highest esteem? You're trying to sell coffins like a market trader. A fucking ugly market trader at that. Sorry about the language, May."

"I'll not stand here and listen to you hurl insults in front of May and her dead son."

"May? Don't pretend you know this woman. You just heard me call her by her name. Have you no shame?"

Bart the bastard was undeterred. "I'll not be offended. I'll put your hostilities down to not thinking straight in a wretched situation. I'll beg leave and be on my way."

Bart walked towards the door. Before leaving, he reached his hand into his upper breast pocket and took out a card. He walked over to May and placed the card beside her on the table.

"I'll leave you this, May, in case you require my services. At the minute, we are doing a special on Amber veneer with a lovely velvet…"

Ted stood up and reached out to grab Bart by the throat, but Bart got to the door before Ted got to him. He was gone.

"The frigging cheek of him, May. Have you ever seen the likes?"

"Ah, Ted, don't let him annoy you. He's only trying to make a living."

"You're too nice, May, giving people like that a by-ball. He was way out of order. Are you OK?"

"I'm fine, Ted."

Ted and May sat chatting. About ten minutes after Bart left, the door opened again. The porters walked in and took Jacky away. Ted and May walked the corridors to the exit. It didn't seem as if anyone else died that night, or maybe they did, but Ted and May saw nothing to suggest this. Then again, nobody saw Ted and May either.

As they got into the car, they started putting their seatbelts on.

"Let's get you home, May. You've a funeral to prepare."

"Yes, Ted, let's go home. I have to prepare."

It wasn't the funeral May was talking about when she said she had to prepare. She had to prepare to live her life without her life, Jacky.

CHAPTER TWO
FRANKY MURPHY

How do I describe Franky Murphy? He wasn't tall, he wasn't small. He wasn't fat, he wasn't thin. I suppose the word I'm looking for is average. In fact, everything about him was average. Except one thing: moaning. This man could moan. He moaned and complained about everything. Now in his late forties, he found something new to moan about every day. It was the boys in the tea hut at work that got the brunt of his whining. Whatever he had watched on TV the night before would be lamented upon the following morning. The younger generation got it the most.

"These young ones these days accepting zero-hour contracts... we're all fucked," he would grunt most mornings at the first mention of a kid starting work somewhere. "As long as they get their drink and drug money for the weekend, they don't care."

He was also a bit daft. He would talk about kids in McDonalds or call centres on zero-hour contracts as morons without realising that he himself, as a self-employed builder, was on a zero-hour contract and had been for years.

He was by no means skint. Being a bachelor all his life, he wasn't short of a few quid. He more than likely stayed a bachelor to save money. He was also a tight-fisted git. Franky wanted respect. He especially wanted it from the young ones he constantly criticised. He wanted the youth of today to abide by his moaning. Tight-fisted shit. They didn't. Franky got all the respect he deserved: none. You only needed to spend a short time with Franky and you would realise that whatever he was talking about was inconsequential to the listener. Franky liked to tell people how funny, brave or intelligent he was, but spend a minute in the man's company and you knew he was the opposite. He wasn't bad, as in evil. I suppose he was just selfish. He was the only one on the planet who mattered, that was the way he rolled.

It was little known, believe it or not, that Franky fancied himself as a stand-up comedian. He had never performed anywhere, except in front of a mirror, but he thought he was the best. He would be discovered one day, although how a talent agent would ever wander into Franky's living room and catch him doing his act in front of the mirror is anybody's guess. He knew this. He wasn't going to get discovered unless he started doing his act in front of people. So, he decided he would do just that, the first chance he got. This would be hard for him because he had lost his faith in human nature. He hated women – maybe that's a bit strong. He had a dislike for women. He would never admit this to anyone. He wouldn't moan about women in case anyone thought it was an admission of his 'gayness'. He wasn't fond of the gay community either, by the way. When asked about his love life, Franky would just say, "I haven't met the right one." How did he lose his faith in human nature though? It all came about when he let his guard down one day while taking his tea break with big Tam, a workmate. The conversation came quite out of the blue.

Sat in the tea hut, Franky and Tam were having a late tea for some reason, and they were alone. As they sat alone, not even talking to each other, Tam farted.

"For fuck's sake, Tam, any chance? I'm eating here," moaned Franky.

"What?" Tam replied, giving Franky a dirty look. Tam was eating a roast beef and garlic mayo sandwich. Half the mayo had made its way out of the sandwich and was now resting on Tam's chin.

"Farting when I'm eating, Tam, farting when I'm eating. I don't fart when you're eating so I would expect you to return the compliment. It's only manners... just manners."

Tam wasn't a bad big lad but he wasn't one for listening to Franky Murphy whinging. "Well, if the truth be told Franky, you don't fart at all, do you?"

The garlic mayo had now built up on Tam's lips as well as his chin and, with him just farting, Franky was disgusted. He had to avert his eyes from Tam's mayo-soaked face.

"I do fart, I just don't fart in public," Franky replied.

"Oh, you're a private farter, are you? I'm a public farter. So what?"

The build-up of sauce on Tam's face was now making Franky ill. He tried take his mind off it by questioning himself as to whether mayo was a sauce or a dressing. Sauce or dressing? Could I use this in my stand-up, he thought.

It was no good though. Nothing he thought of caught his attention more that the white stuff on Tam's lips and chin. He would have to leave or ask Tam to clean it off, preferably with bleach and sandpaper. He couldn't ask Tam to do that – he couldn't risk offending him. Tam was too big, and wasn't one for taking shit. Franky would risk getting a slap.

Franky decided to divert his eyes from Tam, finish his sandwich quietly, and leave. Just as Franky took the last bite of his sandwich and was about to leave, Tam said something that took Franky back a little.

"Anyway, Franky, why do you never talk about women? I know you're not gay, you used to go out with some bird... what did you call her?"

Franky couldn't believe what he was hearing. This stupid, big bastard had hit the nail on the head. It's a coincidence, he thought. But how could it be? How could he mention Laura straight after talking about farting? Could he know her? There's no way she would ever be in this Neanderthal's company. Where could she have met him? She was too nice to haunt any of the shit holes he would go to. How could *that* beast ever be talking to Laura? The paranoia kicked in. Franky had to find out. He had convinced himself in the last ten seconds that Tam had met her, that he was talking to her and that they had a good laugh behind his back. Franky was wrong, it was just coincidental. But Franky was sure they had met somewhere. He had to tell his side of the story. Just in case they had met somewhere, somehow.

"Are you talking about Laura?" Franky asked. His mind was going into overdrive, and he felt a mixture of curiosity and dread. He was curious as to the connection and dreading what the connection might be.

"Aye, Laura, that's her name. Whatever happened to her?" replied Tam, ignorant of the panic going through Franky's mind at that moment.

"You tell me. You must have been talking to her."

"What are you talking about?" answered Tam. "I've never even met her." Franky would never call Tam a liar to his face. Fear of the big man's wrath ensured that.

"Well, just in case you *were* talking to her," said Franky, "I'll tell you the real story."

Franky had bit. His own suspicious mind and his own insecurities had now led him to tell a casual workmate a secret he had kept for years. Tam had now wiped the mayo from his chin and lips in anticipation of the story Franky was about to tell. Unfortunately for Franky, it was now on Tam's sleeve. Franky had to divert his eyes from Tam's sleeve. He proceeded to tell the story.

"I started going out with Laura when I was about fifteen. We were inseparable. I would have done anything for her, given her anything. I hated to see her unhappy or uncomfortable."

"Nothing wrong with that Franky, you were young and in love. It's the way it gets you. One time…"

"Can you let me finish my story, Tam? Just to get the record straight?"

"Sorry, Franky, go ahead. I'm interested. Let's hear your side of the story."

Although Tam had no idea what he meant by his side of the story, he definitely was interested. Franky continued.

"Sometimes Laura and I would go for a meal and then head to the pictures, or the *cinema* as they call it now."

"Do they not call it the pictures anymore?"

"That's irrelevant, Tam. Do you want me to finish the story?"

"Sorry, Franky, carry on."

"Well, we were standing in the queue outside the cinema and some dirty bastard let one rip. The smell was rancid, no… putrid! Like a dead animal. I look around to see if I could spot the dirty bastard who dropped it, and I noticed Laura had a big red face and was close to tears. I realised it was her who farted."

"Laura? *Your* Laura? Laura was the dirty bastard who farted?"

"Yes, it was Laura. It was Laura who farted… and don't be calling her a dirty bastard."

"You said some dirty bastard farted, and it turned out to be Laura. It was *you* who called her it."

"OK, OK. Are you going to let me tell the rest of the story? Or are you going to keep interrupting?"

"Sorry, Franky, must be hard for you. Go ahead, finish the rest of the story."

"I didn't give a flying fuck that she farted, even though it was stinking, but I was embarrassed for her. She was so humiliated. I tried to console her but she was having none of it. After a while, I stopped trying to comfort her about it and decided to never mention it again."

"Is that it, Franky? Your bird farted in the queue at the pictures? Not much of a story, that."

"Let me finish. Even though it wasn't mentioned again, I couldn't get it out of my head. Her embarrassment, her wee red face. I had to do something to make her feel better. I had to even up the score. I wanted to do the right thing."

"Aw, Franky, what did you do?" Tam was busting to hear now. He knew Franky was a silly bastard.

"I waited until we were in another large queue – at McDonalds, actually – and hatched my plan."

"Fuck, Franky, what did you do?"

"Well, I seized the moment and let one rip. In front of everyone. Lifted the leg and everything."

"What in Jesus's name did you do that for?"

"To make her feel comfortable."

"What? Feel comfortable? How's that going to make her feel comfortable?"

"I wanted to show her that I fart, too. We all fart and it can happen any time, any place."

"Franky, I never went to school a day in my life, and even I know how ridiculous that is."

"I know that now, I was just trying to do the right thing. Hindsight's a wonderful thing."

"No, Franky, you don't need hindsight to see how stupid that was. What happened anyway?"

"We sat down, she got a quarter pounder with chips and a portion of onion rings."

"Christ, no wonder she was farting."

"Once, Tam. She farted once. Are you trying to be smart now?"

"No, sorry, Franky. I'm listening. You sat down with your food…"

"Her face was redder than the time she farted. It stayed red, right down to the last onion ring. When she finished that last onion ring, she was gone. Never saw her again."

"You never saw her again? That was harsh! Because you farted?"

"She said she was feeling a little queasy, after the meal. She said she would ring me later that night. She never did. Thinking back, maybe she *is* a dirty bastard – not for farting, but for ditching me like that."

"Didn't you try to contact her?"

"I did but she would tell her ma to say she wasn't in when I called at her house, and the same when I rang."

"That's shocking, Franky. Talk about double standards. You let her get away with public farting but then when *you* public fart, she dumps you? That's just wrong."

"What was the story she told you?"

"Who?"

"Laura. Where did you meet her anyway?"

"What are you talking about? I've never met her."

"What do you mean? How did you know I used to go out with a girl called Laura?"

"I didn't. You asked me if I was talking about Laura, so I just said yes. Never heard head nor tail of her until just now."

Franky realised he had made a blunder. A horrendous error. He wanted no one to know about this – he'd be the laugh of the job, they would go on about it forever. He had to implore Tam not to mention.

"Tam, you and I have been mates for years. I'm asking you not to tell anyone this story. I only told you because I can trust you. The lads, for fuck's sake, I'll never hear the end of it."

"Don't worry, Franky. Not a soul. My lips are sealed."

Franky's faith in human nature, heart-to-hearts and confiding in people, was crushed that day. We could say that maybe this was the catalyst for his cynical view of the world, but it wasn't. He was a dour pessimist before this, but I suppose this reiterated his views. After leaving the tea hut, Tam went straight up to the engineer's office. Tam told the engineer the story. The story was typed, printed and posted on every wall on the building site.

Another thing about Franky was that he couldn't understand why adults who were abused as kids would moan on and on about it. Suck it up, he thought. He was often confronted about this opinion but he had what he thought was an ace card up his sleeve. Franky himself reckoned he was abused, therefore he was entitled to any opinion he desired on abuse victims. Whether or not Franky Murphy was abused is a matter of opinion.

In Belfast in the seventies and eighties, there was a lot of regeneration. The old cobbled streets and the tenement houses were being deserted. New housing estates were popping up everywhere and, for long periods of time, streets were left derelict. These of course were where the children made their adventures. Children spent hours in these derelict houses. They knocked down load-bearing walls, lit fires, made traps, climbed the rooftops, and even scaled the crumbling walls. They were a massive adventure playground for us. Seven, eight and nine-year-olds these days would surely never be allowed near such perils.

When Franky was young, he was always trying to devise games to get attention from the other kids. Let's say he wasn't really liked and was always on the lookout for ways to impress his peers. As he lived near the river lagan, he and others of his age used to collect crabs. Not big crabs – the only crabs that could be found in the lagan were at their biggest about the size of a ten pence coin, but usually more like the size of a twenty pence coin. The children went down to the river bank and would find these little creatures underneath stones and wood when the tide went out. Some would keep them in a wee box as a pet, only to find them dead from suffocation hours later. Some would just let them go in the hopes of finding a bigger one. One day, Franky had an idea. He had found a decent-sized crab and had gotten all the younger children to gather round. The children were excited. He brought them to a small, concrete slab that was sitting by the river bank. As the children gathered, they could see a square box chalked on the slab. Inside the box were four more boxes, dividing the bigger box into quarters. In each of the four boxes, *L, L, D, D* were chalked. He asked the younger children about their catches of the day. Had any of them caught any crabs? Did they still have them? The children were reluctant to give up the spoils of their labour until they knew exactly why he wanted to know. Franky explained.

"We put the crab in the middle of the four boxes, if it ventures into either of the Ls, it lives. If it ventures into any of the Ds, it dies." It was that simple.

Now as adults, we know reason. If we keep the crabs and don't place them in the box then the crab lives, therefore why gamble? But as we also know, children of that age have no such reasoning and a few came forward with their crabs. The crabs had no chance. None of the kids wanted the crab to go into L. The game was pointless. If the crab by luck ventured into L, it was quickly nudged into the D and swiftly stamped on.

There was also the catching of street pigeons. They would get a cardboard box, a small stick, a piece of string and piece of bread. They would tie the string to the stick, place the stick in such a way as it held the box up in a tilt. This would be placed in the middle of the street with the broken-up bread scattered underneath the box. They would then sit out of sight holding the other end of the string. An unknowing pigeon would start eating the bread and would then venture to the bread underneath the box. Once it did, the string was pulled, the stick came with it, the box dropped and that pigeon was trapped underneath the box. The bird was usually set free but the joys of the catch were exquisite.

Franky participated in the trapping of the birds for years but one day, he had a masterplan. Children, as they did with the crabs, always wanted bigger than the last catch. As they lived near the river, there were a lot of seagulls around, but they must have been smarter than the pigeons because none were ever trapped. Franky had a plan. He spread the word one day that he was going to catch a seagull and that everyone had to go to the riverbank at 3pm. Word spread like wildfire. All the kids in the area made their way to the river only to find Franky sitting with a box a rope and a half pound of sausages. Even children at that age knew this was ridiculous. He was laughed at and taunted incessantly – not just for one day; it went on for months. This may have been the catalyst for no one ever taking him seriously again.

Getting back to the question of whether Franky was abused or not, he says he was. Others may have opposing opinions.

****

Franky was out on his own one day. He was flitting in and out of the derelict houses when an older boy accosted him and brought him to the living room of one of these houses. The older boy stripped Franky down to his Y-fronts and for the next four hours made Franky his slave. Nothing serious, go fetch me this boy, go fetch me that boy. Franky obliged. The older boy never touched him though – in fact, the boy was only about a year older than him. It was more tomfoolery if anything, or maybe bullying, but as Franky was stripped to his Y-fronts, he insists he was abused. That day after four hours, Franky made his escape. He bolted from the house, in his underwear, straight round to his own house which was a couple of streets away. As Franky got to the door of his house, his father, Jimmy was walking out. On questioning Franky, and through whatever Franky told him, Jimmy ascertained that his son was sexually abused by an adult. Franky felt in no way violated but exaggerated the story to get his own back on the other boy. Jimmy, not one to take things concerning his children lightly, grabbed his son by the ear and marched him round to the boy's house. There were only the boy's elderly parents at home, one came to the door, then the other, declaring that their son wasn't at home. This wasn't enough for Jimmy. He pushed his way in, searching and wrecking the place in his quest to find the boy. When unsuccessful, he left the place, not without telling the elderly couple that if he ever saw their son he would be dispensing swift justice in the form of his boots and fists. Bummer,

Franky thought. After a long, hot day slaving in his Y-fronts, it would have been nice to see his father batter someone.

****

Twenty-five years later, Franky had forgotten all about this incident, except when he would conveniently remember to cite it when victims of abuse were on TV and he was being chastised for not caring.

Work was slow, Franky had just finished a job and was looking for work. The boy who had stripped him to his Y-fronts that day was now a sub-contractor and was looking for workers. Franky didn't care who it was, he needed money and would work for Satan himself if the price was right. The older boy who had enslaved Franky all those years ago was called Cecil. Franky Murphy and Terry Campbell had been working for Cecil for about three weeks now and they hadn't been paid a penny. They had made an agreement to be paid every week. After the first week, Cecil insisted that the deal was that they would be paid fortnightly. It was accepted by Franky and Terry that there had been crossed wires and they agreed fortnightly. The wages weren't there the second week. Cecil made an excuse that there was a mix up at the bank and that they would be paid three weeks in full at the end of the third week. The Friday they were to be paid, there was still no money. It was time for a showdown.

They had somehow got hold of Cecil's address. Cecil was quite aloof at handing out his address but Franky and Terry had managed to get it. He lived in a tower block. Not a *Trump Tower* tower block. No, this building looked like it was dropped from a helicopter and managed to stay erect. It was a complete dump. Franky and Terry stood at the bottom of it, looking up at it, wondering how they could be working for someone that lived in a rat-infested shit-hole like the one they were looking at.

"Why has this place not been condemned?" Terry asked Franky, shaking his head.

"They can't. The Brits can see the whole of Belfast from the roof. They just land there in the helicopter, set up base and spy on everyone," answered Franky.

"What are you on about, Franky? The British army have long gone from these flats. They may have flown in and set up base in the seventies and eighties, but they're not up there now."

"How do you know? Do you believe everything the British government tell you?"

Franky was annoying Terry and they had only just arrived. "No, Franky, I don't believe everything the British government says, but I think someone, somewhere, would see a helicopter flying onto a roof. And anyway, even if they were still up there, they could still condemn the flats and move everyone out into new homes."

"Just give them new homes? Just move them out and give them new homes? Shower of lazy bastards. It would be handier if they went out and got jobs to pay for their homes."

Terry had heard enough. He was here to collect the money he was owed; not stand and debate the welfare state with an imbecile. "Come on, let's head up and see if he's in."

They scaled the urine-drenched stairwell. Franky, of course, whining about the smell the whole way up. They arrived at the front door of Cecil's flat.

"Are you sure this is the right flat?" Terry asked Franky.

Both men were out of breath after their hike.

"This is it. Definitely. Six hundred and forty-one." Franky answered.

"Are you one hundred per cent sure this is it, Franky?" Terry asked again after ringing the doorbell half a dozen times.

"It's definitely the right one."

"How do you know? Who gave you the address?"

"Fella down the bar gave me the address. It's definitely the right door, put your foot to the door."

"A fella down the bar gave you the address? We're about to kick someone's door in on the say so of some drunk in a bar?"

Franky was adamant that this was the place they were looking for. "He's not just some drunk from the bar. He was here before. He worked for Cecil, too. He got caught for four week's wages."

Terry was disgusted. How could he ever work for somebody called Cecil? In all his working days, he never knew anyone on a site called Cecil. He should have smelt a rat. Hindsight's a wonderful thing, he thought to himself as he lifted his size ten to kick the door in. Before his foot made contact with the door, he was stopped in his tracks by the sound of a frail, old voice behind him.

"What's going on here? What are you doing at that man's door?"

An old lady was stood in the damp, dirty hallway. She wore bedroom slippers, a frock and an apron. Both men looked around at her.

"Go back indoors, love," Franky said. "It's army business. Irish Republican Army business."

The old lady wasn't impressed. "Where are your badges then?"

"What are you talking about, badges? We don't carry badges. We're not Miami Vice, for fuck's sake!" Franky answered dismissively, trying to be funny. He wasn't.

"Mammy vice? What's that? I just want to see your badges."

It was Terry's turn to speak. "Listen, love, you old bat, go back inside. Close your door and mind your own business."

"Don't call me an old bat! I'm not going back inside. You were about to kick that man's door in."

"Listen, missus, go back inside–" Franky's words were cut short by a massive thud, quickly followed by severe throbbing coming from the side of his head. As he cupped his hand over his ear he looked down and lying on the floor beside him was a rather large potato. "What the fuck? Did you just hit me with that potato?"

The old lady had indeed hit Franky on the head with her half-peeled potato. She remained defiant. "Get away from that door or I'm calling the police."

"Go ring the police, we've done nothing wrong," retorted Terry, now trying to hold in the laughter at Franky getting belted with the spud.

"OK, I will."

Franky and Terry watched as the old woman turned and proceeded to walk to her door, which was ajar. Both men now realised that they would have to get out of there fast, especially if the old bird happened to mention the IRA on the phone; the place would be surrounded in a matter of minutes. As they were about to scarper, they noticed that the old lady didn't go back into her flat to use the phone. Instead, she closed the door and started walking towards them again. She was walking at a snail's pace.

"Right, you two, stay there. There's a phone box at the bottom of the street. I'll phone from there."

The two men looked at each other in disbelief. It would take this old woman at least an hour to get to the phone box at the speed she was going. As soon as she was out of sight, the size ten was produced again and the door was kicked in.

As they entered the flat, they both got attacked by the smell. It was a damp, fusty smell, not dissimilar to the smell of the stairwell they had just climbed. The flat was untidy. There was very little furniture. A chair, bed, chest of drawers, scattered takeaway boxes and some empty beer cans.

"Thought you told me this guy had a few quid," questioned Terry, looking around the place in disgust.

"I thought he had money. He always called to the job in a big car, always had a few quid on his tail," Franky grunted, as he started rummaging through the drawers.

"Jesus, Franky, had you no idea he was skint? How could you not tell?"

"What would you like me to do, Terry? Ask to see his bank balance? His credit union book?"

As the two men bickered, they continued to search the flat, trying to uncover some sort of payment for their labour. Cash was preferable but anything of value would be taken. It would then be sold or pawned. There seemed to be nothing though. As Terry looked in and around the bed, he noticed some documents stacked underneath it. He pulled out the pile of official-looking papers, sat on the bed and started reading. As he read the documents, his face started to contort because, if the smell of the flat wasn't disgusting enough, what he was reading definitely was.

Franky noticed him reading the papers. "What is it, Terry? Bank statements?"

Terry sat silent, flicking through the pile of papers.

Franky suspected that what Terry was reading was of interest. He stopped what he was doing and asked again. "What is it Terry? What did you find?"

"He's a fucking pervert," Terry answered lowly, still reading the documents.

"He's a *what*?" asked Franky, who for a split-second thought that Terry might be in possession of pictures taken the day of his slavery.

Terry continued. "These are court depositions. Listen to this." Terry started reading aloud from the writing in front of him. "We gave Martine a doll. We asked her to do to the doll what her daddy does to her. Martine proceeded to pull the panties off the doll. She then started to kiss the doll on the lips." Terry was disgusted at what he was reading. "*Fuck* this shit." He threw the papers to the floor. He was horrified by what he had just read.

Franky, on the other hand... "Nice one, that's a result."

"What are you talking about?" Terry was confused at Franky's reaction.

Franky explained. "Well, if he doesn't give us the money he owes us, we can threaten to expose him. He'll definitely pay up then."

Terry was furious. "Are you for fucking real? He was molesting a child. A guy we know. A guy we worked for. He was interfering with his daughter and you want to use that as collateral? Have you no scruples whatsoever?"

"All right, all right, keep your knickers on. I'm just saying that we have one over on him, that's all."

"Listen, Franky, if I ever get hold of that bastard, money will be the last thing on my mind. I'm surprised by you, where's your sense of decency?"

"Hold on a minute. Don't get on your high horse with me. I was abused as a kid too you know, I know what it's like. And by the very same person."

Terry was genuinely surprised to hear this. "What? You were abused by Cecil? Are you not older than him?"

"No, I'm not! He's older than me. What the fuck makes you think that?"

"I don't know, you just look older. Sorry to hear that, Franky, did he ride you?"

Franky was getting angry at the age mix up and the fact that Terry suggested he had intercourse with Cecil, inferring some type of homosexuality. "Fuck no, he didn't ride me."

"Did he make you ride him?"

"No, he didn't make me fucking ride him. What's the matter with you?"

"Did he touch you, the dirty bastard?"

"No, he didn't touch me."

"Then how did he abuse you?"

Franky wanted to play the victim and tell an elaborated story but he hadn't the time. The police could be here at any minute.

"It's a long story. I'll tell you later."

The two men left with no money and nothing of any worth. All Franky left with was a sore head, courtesy of a half-peeled, over-sized potato. As they got out into the street at the bottom of the flats, they could see the old woman still making her way to the phone box.

****

Jacky had died on the Sunday night. There was a bank holiday the next day, so no one was working. Franky was sitting at home alone on that bank holiday Monday, feeling a little anxious. Usually he would be in bad form because he had lost a day's work due to the bank holiday, but not tonight. He had something on his mind.

Just as he was deep in thought, the doorbell rang. He answered the door and May was standing there. She had a pair of working boots in her hand.

"Hello, May, how are you? What can I do for you?"

"I'm OK, son. Did you hear, my Jacky died last night?"

"I heard something about it, May. He was sick for a while, wasn't he? What did he die of?"

May didn't answer Franky's questions. Instead, she stretched out her hands, offering Franky the boots. "Do you want these boots, son?"

Franky looked at the boots. They were good boots; hardly worn.

"What size are they, May?" asked Franky, taking them out of her hands.

"He was a size ten, son. I thought you might be a size ten. Are you a size ten?"

Franky was ogling the boots, checking the soles, tugging at the laces. He was bad, but not bad enough to start sniffing at the inside of them. He'd have to wait until May left to see if there were any odours.

"I'm nine and a half, May, but they'll do. Extra pair of socks and they'll do rightly. Good boots these, May." He was now keeping them out of arm's length from May, in case she changed her mind because they weren't the right size.

"It would be a sin to waste them, son. You take them and make good use of them. Jacky won't be needing them anymore." May started to walk away from Franky's door.

26

Franky was barely listening to May as she walked away. He was still inspecting the boots, but then he thought of something. "Had he any good working coats, May?" He had to raise his voice a little as May was several feet away.

"I don't know, son. His cubby hole is full of working stuff. I'll have a look for you."

"Thanks, May. Don't forget, will you? Winter will be coming soon, I'm sure Jacky wouldn't want it going to waste."

May said nothing else. She walked away slowly. A broken woman who still had the good intentions she always had.

Franky didn't wait until she was out of sight before he was inside giving the boots a further inspection. He wondered how many times Jacky had worn the boots. He couldn't have worn them that much, he thought. He was always off sick. Been on the drink for years, only worked enough to get the cider money up, then he was away on the drink again. He then started to wonder if Jacky had bad feet. As soon as May's back was turned, he smelt the boots. They didn't smell too bad. Alcoholics never have bad feet, he thought to himself. Bad hearts, bad livers, but never bad feet.

Then he had a thought. He had to move quickly; May would be in bed soon. On the way to May's house, he had thought about Jacky. He thought about the last time he spoke to him. Nothing's bringing him back, Franky thought to himself. Shame to waste his stuff. He was half panting when he got to May's. He knocked on the door.

May was surprised to see him. "Hello, son. What can I do for you?"

"Just called to see when Jacky's funeral is, May. Do you know yet?"

"He'll be home tomorrow. The funeral will be Wednesday. Will you be going?"

"Of course, I'll be there. Jacky and I were like brothers."

"Thanks, son. I hope he gets a good turnout. Do you think his work mates will all come?" May was perking up a wee bit, thinking her son would get a good turnout.

"They'll all be there, May, even if I have to drag them there by the feet myself."

"Don't be doing that, son. I don't want any trouble."

"I'm only kidding you, May. You know what Ted's like, chief pallbearer, likes to see them going down before him." Franky was trying to be funny. He wasn't funny.

"OK, son, see you on Wednesday." May started to close the door, but Franky hadn't finished.

"Just one more thing, May, before you go."

"What is it, son?"

"Seeing as Jacky's dead now, I got a wee speeding ticket the other day. Is it OK if I say Jacky was driving?"

May closed the door in his face.

On the way back home, Franky thought that May was a bit rude. She could have at least answered him. Close the door in his face, though? Takes all sorts to make the world go around, he thought. He wasn't that fond of people like that. Her son Jacky wasn't that cheeky – well, not all the time. He thought of the last time Jacky was cheeky to him. It wasn't that long ago. Sunday night. The night Franky killed Jacky.

CHAPTER THREE
KIT KAT CONFUSION

Ted could certainly feel some of May's pain at her son's death. He himself had a son, an only child. Martin was born late in Ted's life. Ted was now approaching his seventies, and Martin was in his early twenties. Ted and Kathleen tried for children all their married life with no joy. That was until Martin came along when they were in their forties. Kathleen died of cancer when Martin was twelve and left Ted to bring up their son on his own.

Of course, Ted didn't bestow the luxuries onto Martin that his mother would have, had she been alive. His mother thought he was a miracle, a gift from god. She spoilt him for the twelve years she had him. Ted was no such sentimentalist. The boy had to work, fend for himself and make his own way in the world. Ted loved Martin as any father loves a son, which is about half as much as a mother loves a son.

Martin hated work. A lot of his friends weren't working and they got by just fine. They got free money from the government and didn't even have to get out of bed for it. This wasn't fair, he thought. Sometimes he'd be having a drink on a Sunday and had to go home early because of work, while his friends could sit and drink all night because they didn't have an early rise. This is what a lot of the young people see. They don't realise the importance of self-worth at that age. People need to produce for society to enable that society to exist. Ted had a grasp of this basic reasoning and had no interest in who had more than him or who was getting handouts. He knew Martin would eventually see this, therefore enabling him to be content with any job he would do, but that would take time. At the minute, Martin was young and annoyed that he had to venture out each morning smart and clean, and return in the evening covered in muck and shit.

Martin hated his father for thirty minutes every day. Ted would shout at Martin to get up for work, he would leave it five minutes then shout again, then again until he heard movement from Martin's bedroom, then he would stop. This usually took half an hour. That was the half an hour Martin hated him. Ted would have Martin's breakfast ready, then Martin would sleep in the van for the thirty minutes it took to get to work. After that, Martin was back to thinking his father was the best in the world.

Jacky had died on the Sunday, but it was now Tuesday; the first day back after the bank holiday. It was a cold and wet morning. Being the youngest of the squad, Martin would usually get sent for the fries around 9:30pm. Martin didn't mind this errand; it got him an extra thirty-minute break. As he strolled down the site, heading to the café in the rain, he had a smile on his face. Martin liked the rain. For some reason, the rain reminded him of his mother, Kathleen. He remembered their holidays in the Isle of Man. It always rained there. It reminded him of when he was young. At the first sign of rain, Kathleen would be out looking for him to bring him home. It never rained at her funeral, so rain memories were good and positive.

Even though the troubles began to fade as Martin grew up, Kathleen never forgot. In the years previously, Kathleen had watched the news every night during the troubles and, although nearly every night there was a murder, sometimes several, it hurt Kathleen the most when the death of a child was reported. It broke her heart. She thought she couldn't have children at the time but, somehow, she could relate to the loss of a child. She was now determined it wasn't going to happen to her family so she kept a close eye on Martin.

As Martin walked out of the site, down the street and past the toilets on his way for the food, he realised he needed a quick visit. The site toilets were filthy. The urinals were blocked up, bin was overflowing; there was even graffiti on the walls…

> *Down the site they came,*
> *Like a squad of Bengal lancers,*
> *One in six were time served men,*
> *The rest were fucking chancers.*

In this public toilet near the café, there were two cubicles. Only one had a door. The cubicle with the door was locked. Outside the locked door stood Tam. He had been on the beer and cider the whole bank holiday weekend. Tam had ran down to the toilet to relieve himself of the toxic waste that had gathered in his belly and, to his horror, the only decent toilet was taken. He stood outside the occupied cubicle, waiting. Patiently waiting. He had stomach cramps and couldn't fart for fear of letting loose. He had resigned himself to going right there, on the floor, if the occupant was going to be longer than another thirty seconds. He had his belt unbuckled and his zip down in anticipation. He couldn't knock the door and ask the occupant to hurry because this would only irk said occupant who would then most likely take even longer.

Just then, he heard the sweetest music he'd ever heard: the chain flushed. *Thank Jesus*, Tam thought to himself. The floor wouldn't have to be soiled after all. The door opened, the occupant was gone, but before Tam knew it, the door was locked again, with him still outside. Martin had breezed right past Tam and got in before him.

"What the *fuck*?" Tam started banging on the door. "Twenty fucking minutes I'm waiting here."

Martin genuinely never saw him. In his rush to get to the toilet, in case he was late with the breakfast, he failed to see Tam standing outside the cubicle. He knew it was Tam hammering on the door. He knew what size Tam was. But he decided to say nothing.

Tam was furious. "I'll give you five seconds to get out of there."

Nothing.

Tam never gave the five seconds. After three seconds, the only toilet that had a door, had a door no more. With one kick, Tam took the door off the hinges. It came crashing down on Martin's head as he sat on the toilet. Tam's massive hand grabbed Martin by the throat and lifted him clean off the toilet bowl. Martin dangled like a rag doll. Tam placed Martin outside of the cubicle, and placed the door against the door-less frame – not for modesty purposes, but simply because it lay on the toilet bowl, and there was nowhere else to put it.

Martin was lucky. Tam's urgent need to take care of his business meant that Martin had been spared, but he had been doubly lucky. As Martin was being lifted from the cubical by the throat, he happened to glance down and notice that Tam's belt buckle and button had been undone. He spotted Tam's underwear. Black, lacy underwear. Women's underwear. This was his saving grace. He now had one over on Tam. Not only would he be spared for this misdemeanour but he could use it for future misdemeanours. Martin left the toilets laughing. You would think that a young man might be scarred for life at such a hideous sight. Big Tam with a pair of black lace knickers on. But not Martin. He took it all in his stride.

There was brutal honesty about Martin. He would say it as he'd seen it. A lot of young lads are like that. As we get older, we tend to refrain from comments that might offend, even though we would dearly love to say them out loud. Not Martin. He was still young; he said it as he saw it.

When he finally reached the café and opened the door, he noticed it was the guy behind the counter was the one with the psoriasis on his arms. Shit, Martin thought to himself, it's the clown with the scabby arms. He stood in the queue and waited his turn. Ten minutes passed before he could finally give his order.

"Two fries with brown sauce, a tin of Coke, and a sausage roll. And watch none of those flaky bits fall off your arms into the food."

The guy behind the counter ignored the insult and proceeded to write down the order. "There's no sausage rolls."

"No sausage rolls? Just give me a bacon sandwich then."

As soon as he ordered, Martin walked over and put some money into the café's fruit machine. He paid little attention to anything other than the fruit machine, until he was called over to collect his order. He walked to the counter and looked at the order. He was confused.

"What's this? Where's the rest?" said Martin, holding only a bacon sandwich in his hand.

"The rest of what? That's your order," said the equally-confused server.

"Where's the coke? The fries?"

"You said just give me a bacon sandwich."

"What? I said just give me a bacon sandwich instead of a sausage roll, not instead of the whole order."

The server was unmoved by his own blatant stupidity. "So, you want me to put two fries on then?"

Even Martin, who wasn't the brightest himself, knew that this was probably the daftness person on the planet. He refused the offer of the fries as he was now going to be late back. His Dad and Franky would be starving. Ah well, it wasn't his fault, he thought. He left the café, unwrapping the bacon sandwich. As he ate the sandwich going back to work, he cursed the guy in the café for not putting brown sauce on the sandwich.

As he approached the building site on his way back from the café, he spotted Tam at the gate. Martin knew Tam would be confronting him. He knew what he'd seen and suspected Tam wouldn't want anyone else to know.

"Come here, you." Tam beckoned Martin over to him.

Martin had tried a ridiculous attempt to saunter on by and ignore Tam, which hadn't been successful. He walked over to Tam. "Well, big Tam, how's things?"

"Don't try to act stupid. You know rightly what's happening. You pushed right past me in the toilets earlier. I near shit myself."

"Oh, that? Sorry, big man, I didn't think you were ready to go. I thought you were just preparing yourself."

"Preparing myself? What are you talking about?"

"I saw those black, lacy knickers, and thought it may have taken you a while to get them off, so I jumped in before you."

"What knickers are you on about boy?"

"The ones you have on right now." Martin reached down towards the upper part of Tam's trousers to give them a tug.

Tam slapped his hand away. "Listen, boy…" growled Tam, now lightly holding Martin's chin and staring into his eyes. "… you tell anybody – and I mean *anybody* – about what you saw, and I'll bitch slap you every time I pass you on this job. Do you hear me?"

"Loud and clear, Tam, loud and clear. Your secret's safe with me."

Martin left Tam at the gate. He was smiling but cautious enough not to let Tam see the glee on his face. He walked a little faster than usual to the tea hut. He couldn't wait to get there so he could tell everyone about Tam's underwear. Martin knew that if Tam found out he had told the boys in the hut what he'd seen, he would kill him. He then thought about Jacky – maybe there would be two funerals that week: his and Jacky's? His thoughts quickly turned to May. Poor May. May had helped him out big time one night. He thought about that night as he strolled to the hut. Only pausing the memory to stop and tell anyone he passed about big Tam's underwear, of course.

Martin was out on the town one Saturday night. He was around eighteen and it was one of his first nights out. He decided he'd had enough so he ventured out of the bar and was looking for a taxi. He was drunk, in high spirits and having a wee sing-song to himself. He wandered down the street singing Bob Marley's *No Woman, No Cry* but was replacing those famous words with 'no soda, no fry' – a play on words that Martin thought was hilarious. No one else did.

As he stumbled down the street, he ventured upon two men having an argument. They were in the middle of the road, pushing and shoving each other. Martin, because he was in good form, decided everyone else should be, too. In his wisdom, he decided to go over and talk to the two men. He would tell them to work out their differences, be happy, live and let live. Maybe it was the peace-loving lyrics of the song he was singing that drove him to this line of thought – who knows – but he decided to step in away. As he approached the two men, one walked away in the opposite direction, leaving Martin alone with the other man.

"Are you OK?" asked Martin, who was facing the man, with just a few inches separating them.

"Who the fuck are you?" asked the man, not taking kindly to someone poking their nose in his business.

"No need for that, fella," Martin assured him. "I'm only over to see if you're OK."

"Why don't you f–" Before he was able to tell Martin to fuck off, a fist came over Martin's shoulder from behind. It was planted straight onto the nose of the lone man on the road. The other man had come back. The man Martin was looking at went down like a tonne of bricks, knocked clean out. Blood spurted from his nose all over Martin. Martin turned to find the other had gone. Bolted.

Martin turned back to the man now lying on the road unconscious, but also saw two policemen walking, almost jogging, over to him. Martin looked at the policemen, then at the man on the ground, then at his blood-stained jumper. He did what anyone would do. He ran.

Martin must have travelled about two miles. The police were relentless in their pursuit. They were mere yards away from catching him a few times, but he would get a new burst of energy and distance himself every time they were nearly on his heels. But they never stopped. As he ran, he thought about stopping and explaining to them the whole situation, that it wasn't him that knocked the guy out. He was innocent. They wouldn't believe him, he thought.

As he continued running, he remembered the stories of the Guilford four and the Birmingham six, and was determined it wasn't going to be him, locked up for a crime he didn't commit. Even the man who got knocked out couldn't say for sure that it wasn't Martin who hit him because the punch came from over his shoulder. Best keep running.

After those few miles, police still close behind, Martin had to stop. He was going to collapse. His heart was going to burst. So, he jumped behind a wheelie bin in a side alley, hiding there motionless as the police were searching. Martin could hear the police on the radio, calling for back-up to help with the search. He was terrified now. Maybe that man was dead?

He had a decision to make. Give himself up and tell the truth, or be caught. They would think he was guilty. Just before he made his decision on the dilemma, behind the wheelie bin, trembling, he heard a back door opening. It was a woman – the owner of the bin. It was his dad's friend, May. She motioned her arm, beckoning him to come in. She got him inside without being seen.

May kept her house nice. She had lived in one of the old two-bedroom terraced houses all her life. She dreamed of a new house, and when she eventually got one, she really appreciated it. She got all the mod-cons she could afford that she couldn't previously fit into her old kitchen: a dishwasher, a large fridge and a washing machine that didn't have to be kept in a shed in the yard. Her house was spotless. Her kitchen, where she spent most of her time, was painted every so often. She had venetian blinds, a table and chairs, and the kitchen had been nicely tiled by Jacky.

"Sit yourself down, Martin." May pointed to one of the four chairs sitting around her table in the kitchen.

"Thank you," said Martin, truly relieved and grateful to see the friendly face. He was still breathing heavily after the longest sprint of his young life.

May closed the blinds so the police couldn't see in. "Would you like a wee cup of tea, son?" she asked, putting the kettle on.

"Any coffee?"

"No, son, just tea."

"Tea will do fine. May, isn't it?"

"Yes, love, May Johnstone. I know your father well. Would you like a Kit Kat?" May sat a packet of Kit Kats on the table in front of Martin.

Martin looked down at the packet. "Have you any mint ones, May? Not too fussed on the plain ones," he said, not trying to be cheeky; just saying what he was thinking.

"No, son, just the plain ones," explained May, completely unfazed by Martin's unintentional rudeness.

"No orange ones?"

"As I say, son, I've only plain. Do you think I'm telling you lies?"

"No, May, sorry. I wouldn't eat a plain Kit Kat. Have you any Wagon Wheels?"

"I have no Wagon Wheels, Martin."

It was the plain Kit Kat or nothing. Martin opened it slowly, as if not really wanting it. May sat on the chair in silence. Martin's jumper was covered in blood but May asked no questions. Martin quietly finished his biscuit. A few minutes passed in silence, then Martin looked down at his blood-soaked jumper.

"Look at the state of my new jumper. Wore it out for the first time tonight and it's ruined."

May sat in silence, looking at Martin.

"I was in town earlier, May, and…"

"I don't want to know, Martin."

May stood up and walked over to the washing machine, opening its door. May then walked back over to the table where Martin sat. "Stand up, son."

Martin stood up, not really knowing why. May pulled Martin's jumper off, over the top of his head, so that she could wash it for him. Once the pullover was off, and before May was able to put it into the machine, Martin drew close into May and started kissing her on the lips. May was taken aback for a split second. She opened the palm of her hand, and with all the might there is in an old woman, she slapped Martin hard across the face.

"*What do you think you're doing?*"

"What the *fuck*?" said Martin, holding the side of his face that had been slapped.

"Why would you try to kiss me? I'm an old woman! I'm near seventy years of age. Are you not wise, Martin?"

Martin was flustered and a little embarrassed. "I'm sorry, May. I'm so sorry. I read the signs wrong. It was an honest mistake."

"What signs? What signs did you read wrong?"

"It doesn't matter. It was just a big misunderstanding. Please don't say to my Dad."

"What signs are you talking about? I brought you in here, gave you tea and biscuits, was about to wash your jumper. What signs made you think I was going to kiss you? Have *sex* with you?"

"When you closed the blinds."

"I closed the blinds because I thought the police may have looked in and seen you."

"Not just that."

"What else? What other signs did this seventy-year-old woman give you, Martin? Tell me. I'm curious."

"You slipped my jumper off."

"I took your jumper off to wash it. Didn't you notice it's covered in blood?"

"And the Kit Kat."

"What about the Kit Kat?"

"No, not the Kit Kat." Martin was sorry he mentioned the Kit Kat now. He was trying to backtrack.

"*What about the Kit Kat?*"

"Nothing… it doesn't matter about the Kit Kat."

"How on God's Earth could a Kit Kat be a sign? Tell me."

"Sort of… sort of, the two fingers. I thought it was a wee hint."

As far as May was concerned, he had said all he needed to say. This kid isn't the full shilling, she thought. This calmed her. Poor child can't help it. He needs help. Why did Ted never mention his son was a bit backward?

"Go on up to the bathroom, wash the blood off your face. This doesn't mean go to my bedroom and wait on me, by the way. This isn't a sign."

"I know, May, and thank you."

"Get washed, put one of Jacky's coats on and go home. The police have gone."

"Thanks, May. You won't be telling the old fella' about this, will you?"

"Just go, son. I'll have your jumper washed and pressed in the morning. I'll bring it down when your dad's not home."

Martin cringed a little thinking about that night. Ah well, he thought, nothing ventured, nothing gained. May's loss. He had more pressing problems at the minute, though: telling the boys that there was no breakfast.

CHAPTER FOUR
TAM'S UNDERWEAR

Tam was a victim of the madness that enveloped Belfast in the seventies. An IRA bombing and shooting campaign against the British occupation saw many innocent people lose their lives. As a result, Tam was one of the 1,874 nationalists that were interned. Internment was when the British Army would arrest and detain anyone they suspected of involvement in violence, without trial. They would be held in prison camps on the outskirts of Belfast. This was known as Long Kesh.

Tam had no affiliation to any political persuasion. How his name was thrown in the hat to be interned was anybody's guess. Maybe association, mistaken identity – who knows – but he had never any liking nor dealings with the IRA.

When the army came for Tam that morning, it didn't go smoothly for them. As was standard at the time, they arrived at 5am in the morning and rammed the front door, taking the door and the walls that held the door with it. They would rush into the house, then grab, beat and drag that person into the vehicle. The person would not be seen by their family for quite some time.

As four British soldiers tried to drag Tam downstairs, Tam kicked one of them and shouted, "Go back to your own country."

A black soldier responded. "This *is* our fucking country!"

Quick as a flash, Tam answered, looking at the black soldier. "It's hardly *your* country. I can't see any banana trees."

This racist comment incensed the squaddies – well, incensed one of them anyway. Another three joined the four that were struggling with Tam and set upon Tam. He spent six weeks in hospital before being shipped to Long Kesh where he would spend another seven months before being released without trial.

Tam took solace in the thought that he had removed an eyeball from the socket of one of the soldiers during the fight. He couldn't be one hundred per cent sure that he had, but he was ninety per cent sure. This was enough for him to believe that the seven months inside Long Kesh were not in vain.

Tam was only slightly concerned about Martin seeing the women's underwear he had on. He didn't care what anybody thought about him. He didn't want people to know simply because he couldn't be bothered listening to the innuendos, puns and fly comments. Not only that, but if someone annoyed him and he was in a foul enough mood, he might end up in prison. He had been wearing the same – yes, the same – black knickers for years. He loved wearing them. He had a genuine attachment to them, like one would have with a pet. One time, wearing the underwear came to his rescue, saved him from quite an embarrassing situation and even saved him from getting sacked from his job.

****

At least fifteen years ago, Tam was working out in the country, when he got caught short. He was always getting caught short, as you may now have guessed. A combination of cider, junk food and a basic lack of nutritional knowledge made his bowel movements unpredictable. There was no toilet on the farm he was working at this day, so he took a walk to find a place to release what we can now refer to as: his toxic waste. He came across a stable – quite a filthy stable. There was manure everywhere, lots of straw, rubbish, and it smelt rancid. There were a row of stalls in this stable, all containing a horse each. At the end of the stalls, there was a toilet bowl. There was no door, no wash basin, no toilet roll, nothing. Just a toilet bowl. Tam, however, didn't notice that there was no flusher, toilet roll or door. His trousers were down around his ankles and he was in heaven. Better than sex, he thought. Knowing some of the women Tam had slept with, he was probably right.

The complete lack of hygiene in this place didn't worry Tam. What did worry him was that, after he had finished releasing said toxic waste, he decided to look for toilet roll. There was none. He hadn't noticed this, and it was a problem. Being a hot summer's day, he couldn't take the chance of using nothing; he would smart, get scalded, or maybe even blister around his undercarriage. He pondered a few minutes at his predicament, then decided. His underwear. By this time, he had only been wearing this particular pair for five years. They were still very close to him, but he decided that they must be sacrificed. He took off the underwear, wiped his arse with it, and then tossed the sullied garment as far as he could, in the direction of the stalls next to him.

Tam stood up, pulled up his trousers and started to look for the flusher, which, of course, there wasn't one. Just as he did so, the farm owner walked past. He saw Tam and thought it was a good time for a work progress chat. Tam wasn't too concerned that they were chatting beside a waste-filled, unflushed toilet bowl. Why should he be? It wasn't his toilet; should have had a proper flushing mechanism. As he chatted to the farmer, a horse strolled by them. Hanging from the horse's ear, as if carefully placed there, were Tam's black, lacy soiled knickers. The farmer, of course, saw what was in front of him. The farmer looked at Tam, looked at the knickers hanging from the horse's ear, then looked at Tam again. He wrongly ascertained that this big lump of a lad couldn't possibly have anything to do with it. This big man would never wear women's underwear. The farmer was puzzled. Maybe he thought there was a bit of hanky-panky going on with the stable hands? The farmer simply picked up a small stick and lifted the waste-ridden panties off the horse's ear, placing them in the excuse for a bin, just outside the stables. Tam watched as the farmer dislodged them from the horse's ear. He fell in love with them all over again. He felt guilty about discarding them for the sake of his own hygiene. He waited until the farmer left and retrieved them from the bin, placing them in a small plastic bag. This was the day he truly fell in love with the underwear. If he had have been wearing Y-fronts that day, the farmer would have surely known they were his, and he would have lost his job. Never one to forget a good turn, Tam wore the underwear every single day for the next fifteen years, taking them off to wash them on occasion – and those occasions were rare.

****

Martin and the underwear fiasco was not the most important thing on Tam's mind that Tuesday. Tam liked Jacky but loved his mother, May. May and Tam had a unique relationship. Tam had a mother and May had a son, so it wasn't a mother-son relationship, but they were very close. It wasn't anything sexual either. Although Tam had slept with women in their seventies, May never fell into that category. Tam was really worried about May and the effect Jacky's death would have on her. He was worried she might go soon. He had heard before of people passing soon after a loved one, dying of a broken heart.

Tam and May would do a lot for each other. It was Tam who did the decorating in May's house whenever Jacky was on the drink. They would never ask each other for anything, the other would have to offer, that's the way they were. They were getting older now and didn't really need a lot of each other. But it was always nice to know that they were true friends who would be there for each other, no matter what. May was there for Tam when he was younger. It set them up to be friends for life.

****

Tam never had a father to speak of. He was brought up by his mother, Anne. They had very little. Tam didn't care, it was all he knew. He loved his mother dearly and, even at an early age, he knew not to put pressure on his mother for material things. He never wanted her stressed or annoyed in any way. If she couldn't find the money for Christmas or birthdays, he would rather go without than see her fret over it.

It may sound like a cliché – one parent family, no money. Cliché or not, it's the way it is. One parent families are everywhere. The majority struggle. This small family was one of them. But what if the other parent lives nearby with another family? What if he gives the other family everything that a family deserves, but ignores his responsibilities to previous relationships? This is what

39

happened to Tam. Quite content to have a modest life with his mother, he found out a school friend was, in fact, his brother. This friend had all the mod-cons and gadgets while Tam had nothing.

One Saturday night, Tam and his mother, Anne, had gone to bed early. They lived in a terraced two-up two-down. It was nothing special but Anne always kept a clean home. Downstairs there was oil cloth on the floors, on top of which were rugs. There were clean curtains at the windows, a black and white TV, and a coal fire with a fire guard, beside which sat a coal scuttle and a small poker. The upstairs wasn't any more elaborate. Tam's room had a single bed, blankets, pillows and a small chest of drawers. It also had oil cloth on the floor but no rugs or mats.

You could say they were very lucky, just the two of them in this small terraced house. Some houses of the same elk on the street laid home to around ten people, the average being about six per house. The catholic households had a lot more children in them than their protestant neighbours. This was due to the preaching of the Catholic Church about artificial contraception, no doubt. There's no such interest in what the Catholic Church says these days. Back in the day, the old-school parents had their beliefs and it was hard work for anyone who tried to sway them against those beliefs.

On this night as Tam was dozing off into a sleep, he heard his mother scuttling down the stairs. She had heard a knock at the door. It was unusual as they rarely had visitors, never mind visitors at that time of night. Of course, Anne was worried. No good news came at that time of the night. Still in her housecoat and slippers she got to the front door, held her breath and opened it.

"Well, Anne, long time no see."

It was Tommy. Drunk. He was dressed in the fashion of the time – late sixties, early seventies. Flared jeans, tight woolly jumper, baseball boots. He also sported an overly long moustache and long, dark hair that sat just above the shoulders. Unbeknown to Tam at the time, Tommy was his father.

"What the fuck are you doing here, Tommy?" Anne was furious. She wanted nothing to do with this person, sober or drunk.

"I just thought I'd call to see you, Anne. No harm in that, is there?"

"Yes, there fucking is harm in it. Does your wife know you're here?"

"I'm leaving her, Anne, it's not working out."

"What's that got to do with me? I haven't set eyes on you for fourteen years, and you call here, telling me you're leaving your wife. *Fuck off.*" Anne was furious to say the least.

"Has it been that long? Time flies, doesn't it?"

"Do you know how I know it's been fourteen years?"

"How? Did you put it in your diary? Have you been counting the days?"

"Have I, fuck. I last saw you the night your son was conceived."

Tommy was a little taken aback. He called to see if he could brass neck some sex. He was probably passing the house when he had this brain wave, or it was on his mind that night, who knows. Tommy wasn't counting on kids and unimportant things like that getting mentioned. "Oh right, sorry. Can I see him?"

He didn't want to see him. He now knew, however, that he had to act a little concerned about his kid or he would have no chance of sex. The attitude of a drunken man looking for a ride... he would do, promise or say absolutely anything for it. Such delightful creatures.

"Tell me this, Tommy. Why didn't you want to see him on his first birthday? Or his second? Or his third? Or any other birthday? Or Christmas? Or when he was sick?"

"I didn't know, Anne, I didn't know. I've changed."

"You don't know? Well, I know. You weren't looking a drunken ride on any of those occasions because you were with your wife. That's why you didn't call. You don't give a fuck about that boy."

"No, that's not..." Tommy was mumbling now.

Anne was on a roll. "What are you here for, Tommy? A drunken ride? The same drunken ride we had fourteen years ago? Let's go back round to the alley beside the social club where we had sex. Come on, back to the broken bottles and piss-stained walls. It'll be so romantic."

"Do you want to?"

"Fuck off, Tommy. Don't ever call to this door again." Anne slammed the door in Tommy's face.

When Anne turned around, she looked to the top of the stairs. Tam was sat there. He had heard everything. He never asked about his father before. He always thought his father would come for him. He did come, but he hadn't come for him.

Anne could say nothing. To try to sugar-coat it would be insulting to her boy. She told him to get back to bed. He always did what his mother told him, so he did. He lay awake all night, thinking about what he had just witnessed.

Tam, in his young naivety, thought this was the break-through. His dad now wanted to see him. Tam blocked out most of the conversation he had heard and only thought of the words 'can I see him'. What Tam couldn't get his head around was that his best friend, Tom, was now his brother. The man at the door was Tom's dad. He couldn't have asked for a better brother, his best mate.

Anne, before telling Tam to get back to bed that night, told him never to tell anybody what he had heard. He always kept promises to his mother but this meant he couldn't tell his new brother, Tom, that they were brothers. No matter, he thought. Dad will tell him.

A few days passed after Tommy's visit and Tam was on his way to school. His dad, Tommy, was in the distance. Tam walked towards him. As they got closer, Tam was preparing himself on what to say, but Tommy just walked on past him. Maybe he didn't recognise me, Tam thought to himself. A few days later, the same thing happened. In fact, Tommy had probably passed him regularly for years. Tam quickly realised he was being ignored. He hadn't got the gold at the end of the rainbow. He had gotten himself a bucket of shit at the end of this rainbow. Tam had a mind to confront Tommy, but he couldn't. He had promised his mother he wouldn't. He always kept his promises to his mother.

A few months later, it was nearing Christmas. Tam's thoughts of his new-found father had subsided. Fuck him, he thought. If he doesn't want me, I don't want him.

He met up with his mate, Tom –Tommy's son, on Christmas day. Tom had all sorts of gifts: new clothes, a bike, lots of computer games. Tam had very little. He never cared, but this year was different. They both had the same father yet Tom had all the stuff. Why was Tam not getting the same? It really ate him up inside. He still said nothing. He'd promised his mother.

The injustice of that Christmas was put to the back of his mind… until the following Christmas. It all started coming back to him. A year older, a year wiser and a full year of bitterness and resentment.

Young Tom had told Tam that his dad was taking the family to a pantomime. It was a week before Christmas day. This was Tam's opportunity. His opportunity to get his own back and claim what was rightfully his. He waited until the family were gone and sneaked into their house via the back door. He quietly made his way into the parlour area. The bright street lights outside ensured that Tam didn't need any extra lighting to see what was inside. He had ventured into what he saw as Aladdin's cave.

He'd never seen so many gifts under a Christmas tree. He was nervous and had to hurry. He decided not to open them up but to take a chance. He took as many as he could carry in the black bag he had with him. He was panicky the whole way back, but got there without any hitches.

He'd managed to plunder about six gifts. As he started unwrapping them in the solitude of his bedroom, he was perplexed at what he saw. Every one of them was a girly gift. They were for Tom's sister, Lily. Tam had no interest in the gifts: a doll, a make-up set, a hairbrush, amongst others. He hid them under his bed and pondered what he should do with them.

He decided, after a day or two's deliberation, to give them back. He would sneak in again and put them back where he found them. He didn't want the girl's stuff and was frightened his mother would see them. He went around to the house again, after asking his best friend when they would next be out. To his surprise, the back door was open.

Tam never put much thought into what he was doing. He never realised that he was stealing his best friend's gifts. He sneaked back in and put the girly stuff back. He then helped himself to the other presents under the tree.

That's a bit odd, he thought. They've left the door open and left the other presents under the tree after being robbed just a few nights ago. The wrapped gifts he took this time were quite small. He decided to discard the black bag and, instead, stuff the presents into his pockets and down his trousers. On his way home, he got very curious, so he decided to go down an alley to examine the gifts he'd stolen.

May was out and about that night. She had gone to the shop and had stopped off at a neighbour's house. Now she was on her way home. As she passed the alleyway, she could hear vomiting. Curious, she stopped and had a look into the darkness. As she scanned the alley to see what the noise was, she spied Tam, the young lad from down the street. May, not one to walk past anyone in distress, approached him.

"Are you OK, son?"

Tam recognised May, the nice lady from up the street. "I'm OK, Mrs Johnstone." Tam was wiping the vomit from his mouth. At his feet, lay about a dozen chicken heads. It seems Tommy was keen on a little sick humour for the thief, if they returned.

"What's all this?" asked May, looking at the vomit and headless chickens on the ground.

"I don't know, Mrs Johnstone. I was just walking down here and I saw them. It made me sick."

May lifted Tam's hands and smelt them. She knew he had been handling the chicken heads. "Why, Tam?"

"Why, what?"

"Why would you steal those children's gifts?"

"What are you talking about? I didn't steal any gifts."

"Do you know who I was talking to today?"

"Who?"

"Tommy Mac. He told me that the kids' gifts had been stolen. He said that if whoever stole them comes back, they'll get a shock. He told me about the chicken heads. Now you have them. Why, son? Why would you do such a horrible thing?"

"It wasn't me! They were lying here, I…" Tam was interrupted by May's soft voice. A voice of concern. She gently cupped the side of his face with her hand. "Why, Tam? Why would you steal another child's Christmas presents? I know you, I know your mother. You are both good people."

"You don't know what I am."

"You're a handsome young man with a heart of gold, that's what you are."

"I'm a fucking shag down an alley, that's what I am. A dirty, drunken ride. Probably this alley… I was probably conceived against this very wall, right here. I'm more disgusting than those chicken heads and that vomit."

"Don't say that, son. It doesn't matter how you were conceived and it matters not who your father was. It's about who *you* are."

"Why shouldn't I get the same stuff as them? They're my brother and sister. Why should they get everything? I get nothing."

May was furious at this comment. She lifted her hand and slapped Tam across the face – much like the slap she hit Martin with in the following years.

"You get nothing? You get *nothing*? Your mother would die for you. You get all the love and care a mother is capable of. What do you want, Tam? A bike? A computer game? Do you think these things are something? Your mother gives you everything she can and, on top of the things she gives you, you also have her heart and her soul. These two things – the most important things on Earth – you will have for life. You're a lucky, lucky boy, son. Don't ever forget it."

Tam hung his head in shame. He knew she was right. At home, he had everything he ever needed. He didn't need anything from Tommy Mac.

"I'm sorry, Mrs Johnstone."

"You've no need to be saying sorry to me, son. As far as I'm concerned, you made a mistake, but the bigger mistake was made by the man who abandoned you," said May, now hugging Tam.

"I'll go around. I'll admit it was me. I'll apologise."

"You'll do no such thing," scowled May. "You'll go to my house and get washed. There'll be nothing else said about it."

May took Tam home. She washed him, fed him and gave him a couple of pounds. She made him promise to her that he would forget about Tommy Mac. After that night, Tam never thought about having a father again. May brought him a gift every birthday and every Christmas thereafter. Why should he care about having no father? He now had two mothers. He was luckier than them all.

****

Tam called around to May's the night after Jacky died. He left it late. He had good reason. Franky had just left May's door, asking about the speeding ticket. When the doorbell rang again, May thought Franky was back to ask for something else, but he wasn't; it was Tam. He hugged her as soon as she opened the door.

"I'm not long hearing about Jacky. Are you OK?"

"I'm OK, son. You'll not stay long, you've work tomorrow."

"I'll stay as long as you like, May. Who went to the hospital with you?"

"Ted."

"Fair play to him, May. I hate hospitals but you should have given me a shout."

"For someone who hates hospitals, you're going to be spending a lot of time in them yourself with that drink."

"Please, May, don't be starting on me. Do you not think I'm bad enough, what with Jacky dying?"

May noticed Tam was carrying something. "What's that in your hand?"

Tam was holding a slightly bulging Tesco carrier bag. "It's soup, May. I made some. Thought you might like a wee drop."

"Soup? Looks like a block of ice in a plastic bag."

"I had it in the freezer. I cut it in half with a hatchet."

"You cut it in half with a hatchet? Why didn't you just defrost it in the microwave?"

"I don't know how to defrost on that thing, May." Tam set the soup down. He sat on the chair in the living room. May sat opposite.

"Where do you think he'll go, Tam?" May asked.

"Will he not be coming here then? To the graveyard?"

"That's not what I mean. His soul – where will his soul go?"

"Sorry, May. I don't really know. Heaven? Hell?"

"Hell?"

"Did I say hell? No, not hell. I meant heaven."

"I'm not a real believer in all that mumbo jumbo, Tam."

"You're not?"

"Not really, son. It makes you think…"

"What does?"

"It makes you think, if there is nothing after this life, why do we have to bury his body? Why can't I keep it?"

"Now, May, don't be thinking like that. That's ridiculous."

"Why? Why is it so ridiculous?"

"Because he'll start decomposing, May. He'll smell and stuff."

"I don't care about smell. As for decomposing, it wouldn't matter to me. I've seen him before in some terrible states."

"You're better remembering him how he was. Your handsome son. That's how you want to remember him."

"You know, Tam, when I think about him now, I can only see my little boy. Not the sunken-faced drunk he became. That drink… it's a curse. Have you ever thought of going off it, Tam?"

"I have, May, all the time. But the thought of going off it stresses me out, so I take a wee drink to calm me."

Tam went and got himself a couple of bottles of cider. He sat with May until the early hours. He would have stayed longer if it wasn't for May making him go home to get up in time for work. As he closed the door, he was empty inside. He adored that old lady, so how could he, just over twenty-four hours earlier, kill her son?

CHAPTER FIVE
STACEY'S WALK OF SHAME

Stacey had a great wee job on the building site. Every morning, she would give the tea hut a quick clean, fill the boiler, empty the bins and mop the toilets. She loved this wee job. It got her out and about, and the craic was good. Along with her bar job, she got along quite nicely. She didn't have to pour their tea but she always waited on the boys coming in so they could have their tea handed to them.

Stacey wasn't too proud to clean the site toilets. She knew that if it was left to the men on the site to do it, they would end up immersed in their own filth and shit. Stacey was a real feminist. While so-called feminists would moan about why women are cleaning and making tea, Stacey took no heed. Her opinion was that the men worked hard and if someone was paying her to make their tea hut comfortable and clean, then she had no problems with it whatsoever.

Stacey was about five foot, with fair hair and an average build. She was quite attractive and was usually very polite. She didn't like confrontation at all. She didn't fear it; just couldn't be bothered with it.

Stacey, like a lot of women, was a romantic. She had no time for the flowers and chocolates but she believed in moments and memories. She always believed there was a soul mate for everyone somewhere. Some would find that soulmate; some wouldn't. She had found hers. Unfortunately for Stacey, it didn't work out as it does in the films. The romantic notion of happy ever after rarely came to fruition. Stacey's soul mate was Jacky Johnstone.

He was the love of her life. They hadn't been together from an early age, although they had known each other to nod to and say hello. Stacey netted her prize fish, Jacky, once she knew he was interested in her. They lived together for a couple of years, not long you might think for a couple of soul mates, but Jacky's constant drinking was without doubt the deciding factor in the break-up. He was never violent to her, and never shouted or became aggressive, but Stacey just couldn't watch her only true love disintegrate in front of her eyes. As each day passed, Stacey would see Jacky become less of the man he was the day before. She had moved out a few years back. They still spent time together though, right up until his death, two days previous.

Stacey had decided to go to work on the Tuesday, even though she was devastated. She had to keep herself busy. She had spent the whole of the bank holiday Monday crying. As she was wiping the tea hut sink, Ted was the first in.

"How are you holding out, love?" asked Ted, placing his hand on her shoulder.

"I'm fine, Ted," she lied.

"You and Jacky were still knocking about, weren't you?"

"Now and again, Ted, nothing serious."

Ted sat down. "I was at the hospital on Sunday night with May. Desperate state of affairs altogether. Is that water boiled yet?"

Stacey didn't answer. She was deep in thought. Ted helped himself to the water. It was tearing her to shreds.

Jacky's gone, she thought. What a loss. A real man. If Stacey was ever asked to describe Jacky, that's what she'd say: a real man.

Stacey had fancied Jacky as long as she could remember. She would see him about but lacked that little bit of courage it took to approach him. One day, she bumped into Jacky in the shop. They had some idle chit-chat and small talk. Straight out of the blue, Jacky asked her out for a drink. Stacey couldn't believe her luck. She left the shop in absolute bliss. There was one small problem though: she was living with someone. She was looking for a way to get rid of Billy for a long time. She kept putting it off because she couldn't be bothered with the stress and annoyance so she let it linger on. She couldn't let it linger anymore if she was going to have any sort of relationship with Jacky. Her heart skipped a beat every time she thought about going out with Jacky. She had bumped into Jacky on the Saturday and they were to meet Sunday afternoon. Little did she know that it was to be the worst day of her life.

****

Stacey started to make plans to rid herself of Billy the second she walked out of the shop. She would tell him to pack his stuff when she got home. Before reaching her house, it dawned on her that it was Billy's birthday and they were due to go out that night for a celebration. She had a dilemma. Stacey had a good heart – a heart that wouldn't let her drop him on his birthday; a decision she would come to regret. I won't dump him on his birthday, she thought. We'll go out tonight and I'll tell him in the morning, he'll be out by eleven, just in time for her to get ready to meet Jacky at one.

That morning she lay in bed contemplating what she was going to say to Billy. He was beside her in a drunken stupor.

"Billy, we need to talk."

No answer.

"Billy, we need to talk." Slightly louder.

No answer.

"Billy? We need to talk." She was now shaking him.

Billy started to respond. "Are you making any breakfast?"

He was barely audible. Because of the all-night dribbling from the side of his mouth, his face was stuck to the pillow. Stacey knew that talking now would be futile; it would be like talking to someone on a life support machine.

She decided to feed him first. "What do you want for breakfast?"

"Any vegetable roll?"

"No."

"Beef sausages?"

"No."

"Pork sausages?"

"No."

"Black Pudding?"

"No."

"Bacon?"

"No."

"Fuck's sake, Stacey, is there anything in the fridge?"

"There's eggs and mushrooms."

"Eggs and mushrooms? Is that it?"

"That's it. Do you want them or not?"

"I suppose that'll do."

Stacey went downstairs. By the time she had prepared the food and returned to the room, Billy was sitting upright, awaiting his breakfast. Stacey handed Billy the food: eggs and mushrooms with a cup of tea.

Billy looked down at the plate with a look of distain. "What the fuck's this?"

Billy wasn't a pleasant person. He was chauvinistic and his arrogance stunk. He was in someone else's house, in someone else's bed, eating someone else's food that someone else had prepared. He wasn't grateful in the slightest.

"Eggs and mushrooms," answered Stacey, who wished he would hurry up and eat so she could finish with him. Why she didn't finish with him as he ate is anybody's guess.

Billy was aggravated. "Did you not make an omelette? And what's this? Tea? Is there no beer?"

"Why would you think I was going to make an omelette? I never mentioned an omelette."

"I didn't think it needed mentioning. Who eats scrambled eggs with mushrooms on the side? It's disgusting."

"Give it here, if you don't want it," Stacey said, trying to grab the plate.

"I didn't say I didn't want it." Billy was holding the plate out of Stacey's reach. "I just thought you could have taken the time to make an omelette, that's all."

"It would have taken less time to make an omelette, if you had have asked for a *fucking* omelette."

Billy munched away at his mismatched food. He was mumbling away at his distaste for eggs and mushrooms while shovelling it into his mouth. His mumblings also consisted of how long it would take to make an omelette. As he had never cooked a thing before in his life, and didn't know how long it would take, he decided not to press the point.

Stacey knew he would be asking for sex. Billy asked for sex every morning. In fact, he asked for sex every morning, every evening and every night. Times when she enjoyed sex with this person had long gone – if ever there ever was a time, that is. He wasn't getting any this morning. He was getting dumped. Her days of faking orgasms were over. She would wait until he finished breakfast and tell him.

Stacey sat at the edge of the bed. Her room was nicely decorated. She kept the windows open all day, every day to air the room and would keep it spotless. Sitting there she could smell his feet, stale booze and that stale tobacco smell. She could also smell trapped farts. She suddenly had thoughts of Jacky lying there. She wouldn't care about his boozy breath or trapped farts.

She couldn't wait to get Billy out of the house. But what if he refuses to go? Makes a big deal out of it? They would argue and she would miss her date with Jacky; her date with her destiny. How could she get rid of him easily? Without fuss? He could sit begging for ages, claim his undying love, the usual shite.

It was then that Stacey decided to do the stupidest thing ever. Sometimes, when people are under pressure, they don't think straight, and this was one of those times. She decided to have sex with him. Why? She didn't even like him never mind want to have sex with him. But Stacey's opinion was that a man didn't care much about anything after sex. He would promise you the world, the moon and the stars, just to get his leg over. After the event though, he didn't care much about anything. Men are like this. Billy was like this. They would have sex then, thirty minutes later, he'd be having a pint. If she denied him sexual gratification on this occasion, it could take hours to get rid of him. Stacey hadn't got hours. That's it, she thought, I'll have sex with him, then tell him it's over. He won't care then. He'll have filled his boots and he'll be on his way. So, she had sex with him. And it worked! She broke up with him just after, and Billy was gone, and didn't seem to care much about being dumped. As the rest of that day unfolded, however, she would live to regret it.

That afternoon, Stacey met up with Jacky. They had a wonderful time together. Jacky was everything she thought he was and more. Handsome, funny, kind, courteous. Their first date was a success. Jacky had fallen for Stacey in a big way, too. That afternoon, after a few innuendos and a little giggling, it was a done deal: they were heading to Stacey's to sleep together. At the start of the date, Stacey had made up her mind that this was not going to happen. She had slept with Billy earlier and wasn't like that. After a good day and a few drinks, and what with Jacky being so handsome and sexy, her mind had started to change. She convinced herself that what happened that morning with Billy wasn't sex. It was a transaction purely to unblock the path to Jacky.

Sex with Billy wasn't real sex, she told herself. She had done it for a reason; to get to Jacky. They ended up going back to Jacky's house in the end, and had a *very* special evening.

Jacky was working the next morning, so Stacey left in the early hours. She was on cloud nine leaving Jacky's. She had got the man of her dreams, the man she had always wanted. As she walked the short distance from Jacky's house to hers, she bumped into a friend. Her friend was having a house party and invited Stacey. She wasn't one for these kind of parties; they were a bit boring and predictable. But maybe one for the road, Stacey thought. What harm could it do? Stacey stayed longer at the party than she would have liked. After a clatter of vodka and cokes, she got tired and drunk. Too tired and too drunk to go home. She asked her friend if she could crash in one of the bedrooms. It wasn't long before Stacey was sleeping. Or more like unconscious. Stacey awoke the next morning to every drunk woman's nightmare: a total stranger was on top of her, trying to penetrate her.

As her eyes opened she could see an ugly, unshaven, sunken face about an inch away from hers. She at first felt fear but that quickly subsided into fury and rage.

"Get the fuck off me! Get fucking off me!" Stacey shouted, pushing a drunk Toby Trunks off her.

"What's the matter with you?" asked Toby.

"What's the matter with *me*? What's the matter with *you*, you dirty bastard?" Stacey jumped out of bed. She was fully clothed, but her skirt was pulled up over her thighs, so she quickly pulled it down.

"I was just looking for a wee jump before I headed home. There's nothing wrong with that – a man has to eat," declared Toby, pissed off at the rejection.

"Go fucking eat somewhere else. Why would you think you could do that? Fucking pervert... attempted rape that is... I'm going to the police."

"You weren't saying that a few hours ago, you were all for it, loved it."

Stacey was genuinely taken aback by this comment. "What are you talking about? A few hours ago? What happened a few hours ago?"

"You and me. Great it was, too. You lay like a sack of potatoes though, but I like that. Not usually my type, but as I say, a man has to eat."

"You disgusting bastard. You had sex with me while I slept? I'm going to the police right now." Stacey reached for the door handle.

"You weren't sleeping. You were awake. Well, probably half awake."

"I was asleep and you know it. You'll be getting a rap on your door Toby Trunks, or whatever your real name is – the police will know it. You're probably on the sex offenders register, anyway, perverted fucker."

"Oh? You know my name now, do you?"

"Of course I know your name, Toby Trunks. Soon to be Toby the rapist Trunks."

"If you know my name, why were you calling me Jacky when we were having sex? I wasn't offended, by the way. You could've called me anything and I wouldn't have cared."

"Jacky? Why would I call you Jacky? I know your name."

"I don't know why you were calling me Jacky. I thought you were up to some kinky shit or something. You never opened your eyes. I just thought… well…"

"Well, what? You just thought what?"

"I thought you were being a bit kinky, closing your eyes and thinking I was Jacky Fullerton."

"Jacky fucking Fullerton? Are you serious?"

"Maybe. There are some sick people out there. I know a guy who sits in the corner dressed as an owl watching people have sex."

It was starting to dawn on Stacey; she might not be able to claim rape. In her drunken, semi-conscious state, she thought she was still with Jacky. Her guts were ripped to shreds. She could only muster two more words. "Get out."

Toby Trunks left the house. Stacey left shortly after. She walked home in a daze. She wasn't going to sleep with Jacky; she would never have sex with two people on the same day. Now she had had sex with three people on the same day. She threw up three times, walking the short distance home. A walk of shame like no other. Stacey stayed in bed all day that day. Regret, shame and disgust were just some of her emotions. She eventually got it into her head that no one would ever know. No one would ever find out. She could never tell Jacky, and risk losing the thing she had wanted for so long.

Four weeks had passed since that silly Sunday. For Stacey, calling it silly was the understatement of the decade. Apart from that, things were good. She and Jacky were flying high. He was everything she wanted in a man – he drank a little too much but that would be sorted in time. As Stacey browsed through the aisles of the local supermarket, the memories of that day were starting to fade. Just as she was checking the fat content of various dairy items, she turned around and was standing next to Billy, her ex-boyfriend. He was with his new flame, Lou-

Lou. As Lou-Lou examined the fat content in buttermilk a few feet away, Billy stopped for a chat.

"Didn't take you long, Billy," said Stacey, nodding her head in the direction of Lou-Lou, who was still examining the buttermilk.

"Lou-Lou? Sure, me and Lou-Lou go back a long way."

"That's good, Billy. You two look good together."

That's all Stacey had to say. She went to walk on, but Lou-Lou had clocked her talking to Billy and stormed over.

"What are you talking to that slut for?" said Lou-Lou, talking to Billy, but looking at Stacey.

"Who are you talking about?" asked Stacey, knowing full well who she was referring to.

"Well, I can only see one slut here – a slut who sleeps with two men on the same day."

Stacey was speechless. She didn't know where to look. All sorts went through her mind. How did she know? Does Jacky know? Two? There were three. Which two did Lou-Lou know about? If that mouthpiece knows, everyone surely knows. Lou-Lou smiled a smug grin and walked away from Stacey. The smile quickly vanished when a carton of milk exploded against her head. Luckily for Stacey and Lou-Lou, they weren't in the canned food section. Stacey had hit her over the head with the first thing that came to hand. The milk ruined Lou-Lou's over-exaggerated make up and fake tan. Stacey made her exit from the building while Lou-Lou was screaming profanities at the top of her voice. Stacey heard nothing; she could only hear her own guilt and shame pounding away in her head. She was shaking and fumbling for her keys in the car park when Billy made his way over.

"Are you OK, Stacey?"

Stacey looked at Billy.

"I'm OK. What was that thing you're going out with talking about?"

"I've no idea what she's talking about," said Billy, obviously lying.

"Don't talk shite, what are people saying about me?"

"It wasn't me. It was Toby Trunks."

"Toby Trunks? What was Toby Trunks saying?"

"He was trying to be smart in the bar one day. He said he banged you when you were going out with me. I told him to go fuck himself, but he pulled up the dates and he was right. He had sex with you on the same day as we broke up."

"Oh, Jesus. Did this conversation go on in front of the whole bar?"

"Not really. There were only a couple of us in that day. Monday club. Your boyfriend Jacky stepped in and told Toby Trunks that if he mentioned your name again, he'd be spitting pieces of beer bottle out of his mouth for the rest of his life."

Stacey near fainted upon hearing this. "Jacky? Jacky? He was in the bar when this was being talked about?"

"He was. On a brighter note, I was right – we had already broken up that morning, so he never had sex with you while you were going out with me."

"Fuck off, Billy"

It's hard to know how Stacey could drive that day. She was in a complete daze. If Jacky knows about those two, and he obviously knows about himself, then he knows there were three in one day. Why hasn't he said? Why hasn't he mentioned? He's not stupid, he obviously knows.

On the way back from the supermarket, Stacey remembered that she had money belonging to May. May had given her twenty pounds to get a few things at the supermarket. But, as Stacey had left with nothing, she went to May's to return the money. When she got to May's door, she composed herself. She half opened May's hall door.

"Hello, May? Are you in?"

"Come on in, Stacey," shouted May, who was in the kitchen.

"I'm sorry, May… I didn't get a chance to get those things for you. Here's your money back."

"Don't worry about it, love. Do you want a wee cup of tea? You look a bit flustered, are you all right?"

"I'll take a wee cup, May, thanks."

"Sit yourself down. Did something happen?"

"I'm OK, May, just had a run-in with that Lou-Lou thing."

May got serious. She looked Stacey directly in the eyes. "What did she say?"

"Just nonsense, May." Judging by May's demeanour, Stacey had now twigged that May knew something.

"Don't let anyone run you down, Stacey. Things happen in life, we all have regrets. We certainly can't undo what we have done. We just have to move on."

"What are you talking about, May? Has anyone said anything about me to you? Is *everyone* talking about me?"

"There's no one talking about you, love."

"You heard something, May. I know you did. What did you hear about me?"

May realised she couldn't lie to Stacey. If she lied, Stacey would fear the worst. She decided to tell her the truth. "I'm guessing it's about what happened that Sunday? The Sunday you started going out with Jacky?"

"What Sunday?" replied Stacey, still forcing herself to deny everything, but she knew May knew.

"Jacky told me. He wasn't gossiping – he asked my advice."

"It's all lies, May, all lies."

"It doesn't matter, love. What's done is done. He was worried about you. He didn't know whether he should tell you he knew. He didn't want to upset you but, at the same time, he didn't want to lie to you. I said it was his choice, so he decided not to mention it to you."

Stacey had nothing left to say here. She wasn't prepared to talk about that day; the most shameful day of her life. She had thinking to do. "I've got to go, May. Thanks for the tea." Stacey left the untouched tea sitting on the table and left.

When Stacey left May's, she was devastated. Jacky knew all this time. He never mentioned it, never judged her. He was handsome, loving and funny. He could have his pick of women. He chose to stand by her.

****

From that day on, Stacey knew Jacky was the love of her life – the only man she wanted or would ever want. Stacey was thinking about all this, while preparing the tea hut for the boys' tea break. When they came in, they'd be talking about Jacky. They might ask questions. She had to make sure she didn't talk too much. She could never tell them that she was with Jacky the night he died. She couldn't let them know that she killed the love of her life.

CHAPTER SIX
THE TEA HUT

Franky was uneasy as he entered the tea hut on the Tuesday. He liked to talk a lot and he feared something about Sunday night would come out. Franky tended to talk without thinking, so he had to be careful. He would waffle on and on, moaning, belittling and whining. He was arrested very few times in the troubles. The RUC must have known him, or known about him. Any information they may have got out of him they decided to do without so as not to have to listen to his bullshit. He decided to act natural. He entered the tea hut moaning.

"That has to be the shittiest morning I've ever had on a building site," he whined as he slammed his hard hat on the table. By now, Ted was musing through the paper. Stacey was still at the boiler. Both Stacey and Ted didn't want to know what was on Franky's mind but Stacey was too polite not to ask.

"What's the matter, Franky? Who's annoying you now?" she asked, without looking at him.

"That idiot bricklayer foreman. I asked him, how many of his squad does he think are gay. I explained that I didn't know any gay bricklayers, so they must all be in the closet, afraid to come out. There's gay policemen, firefighters, doctors, sportsmen, yet I don't know one gay bricklayer. Not one. It's disproportionate to the rest of mankind, so they must all be in the closet."

"What did he say?" asked Stacey, still not remotely interested.

"He said, there's no such thing as a gay bricklayer. Eh? No such thing as a gay bricklayer. Bricklayers, as far as he's concerned, are exempt from being gay. It's hard enough trying to do a day's work without having to listen to that shite."

"I'm here to do a day's work and I have to listen to your shite," replied Ted, not bothering to look up from his paper.

"Do you want any tea yet, Franky?"

"No thanks, Stacey. I'll wait until Martin comes back with the fries."

Franky, totally ignoring Ted's previous comment, turned his attention to him. "Ted, do you know any gay bricklayers?"

"I don't know, Franky, to be honest. I've never really thought about it."

"That bricklayer foreman, Ted, he'd put years on you, I swear."

"Why, Franky? Does he think you're gay?" asked Ted, now trying to wind Franky up a bit.

"No, he doesn't think I'm gay. Why would he think I was gay?"

"I don't know, I was just asking. I don't know what you two were arguing about, and you are getting on like a woman."

"I'll tell you what we were arguing about, Ted. He said there was no such thing as a gay bricklayer…"

"Have you nothing better to do out there than to talk about what bricklayers do in the bedroom? How about doing a bit of work, Franky?"

Once Franky's work ethic was questioned, he changed the subject. "Where's Martin with the fries? He's away ages."

"He'll be here soon enough," answered Ted, still not looking up from his paper.

"Is Martin definitely your boy, Ted?"

"Leave him alone, he's only young."

"He's thick as champ, Ted, no harm to you."

"I said leave him alone."

"Do you know what he said to me the other day? Your Martin, do you know what he said to me, Ted?"

"What did he say?" asked Ted, wanting Franky to hurry up and tell him, on the off chance that he might shut up after he explained.

"We were talking the other day about the Americans, how they're all over the world bombing the shit out of people for oil. Do you know what he said, Ted?"

"What did he say, Franky?" asked Ted, still uninterested.

"He said, why do the Americans want all the oil? Would it not be far healthier if they left it where it is and just grilled their food?" Franky waited on Ted's response, but he didn't get one.

"Did you hear what I said, Ted? He thinks the Yanks are going into every country under the sun to rob them of their cooking oil! Crisp and dry, to put in your chip pan. The kids these days, Ted, they haven't a notion."

Ted didn't even acknowledge what Franky said about Martin, either he wasn't listening or he didn't care. He knew the youth of today cared nothing about anything other than the weekends. He was hungry though.

"I wish he would hurry up with the fries… tea time will be over soon," declared, Ted, still not lifting his head from the newspaper.

"I hope he doesn't get served by that boy with the psoriasis who works in the café," moaned Franky.

"Stop it, Franky, the kid can't help what he's got. He's got to earn a living, like the rest of us."

"I'm not talking about his psoriasis, Ted. I'm talking about his stupidity. He's worse than Martin. Do you want to know what he did, Ted?"

"Not really, Franky, I'm trying to read my paper, but I'm sure that won't stop you telling me."

"I needed change for parking the other day. I went into the café to get change for a twenty. He said he couldn't open the till unless I bought something. I said give me a packet of crisps – they were fifty pence. He gave me the crisps and rung in the fifty pence, then he looked into the till and asked me, had I not got fifty

57

pence change. Huh? I mean, Ted, of all the morons, I didn't even want the crisps. I give up on the kids these days. Stupid, just stupid–"

"OK, Franky," Ted interrupted. "You've made your point. The kids these days are stupid. Can I just read my paper now?"

"Big Tam was going to kill Martin earlier, just before he headed off to the café. Something happened in the toilets. I didn't hear the full details."

"Big Tam? And my Martin? Has he been winding that big lad up?" Ted suddenly got interested, and looked up from his paper.

"Don't know what happened, Ted, but I heard Tam was cross... very cross."

"He'll be here soon. He can tell us himself."

"That's if big Tam doesn't get him first."

Ted got serious. "Don't you concern yourself. Tam won't be touching my Martin." Ted then turned his attention to a more serious subject. "You know Jacky's getting buried tomorrow?"

Stacey and Franky fell silent for a couple of seconds. They didn't want to broach the subject but knew they had to.

"Where's he getting buried, Ted?" asked Franky, pretending he cared.

"Rushlawn," answered Ted.

There was another uneasy silence.

Franky broke this silence with a silly question. "Senegal Sam's grave's there, isn't it, Ted?"

"Who knows, who gives a fuck? Nobody's going to visit it anyway," answered Ted, still not looking up from his newspaper.

"I take it you didn't like him, Ted?"

Ted lifted his head from the paper. He gave Franky a stern look. "Take a wild guess."

Stacey was curious about who knew what about Jacky's death. She didn't want to draw suspicion by asking too many questions but she had to know. "Were you talking to May, Ted? What was the cause of death?" Stacey did care about the cause of death. She cared much more than she let on.

"I didn't ask her, Stacey. I just assumed it was the drink. He'll not be home until later. Because of the bank holiday yesterday, she'll only have him in the house for one night, before he gets buried tomorrow. She couldn't get a slot later in the week."

Stacey knew Jacky's body hadn't come back to May's yet. She was relieved at what Ted had just said. Stacey thought they were doing a marathon autopsy on him. "Oh, they couldn't release him because of the bank holiday? I thought they were doing tests... or something... to find out the cause of death."

"That's all I know, Stacey. It was because of the bank holiday," confirmed Ted.

"I might give the funeral a miss, Ted. We're a bit busy in here," declared Franky.

"You'll be taking the day off for his funeral, Franky." Ted said. "No ifs or buts."

"I wouldn't really call him a friend, Ted. To be honest, I had a bit of a fall out with May last night after she brought his boots over."

Ted looked at Franky's face, then down to his feet. "Are they Jacky's boots you've got on?"

Franky got defensive. "And what? May brought them over last night. I didn't really want them... just took them to be polite, if I'm honest."

"Jesus, Franky. Could you not have waited until the man was buried before wearing them?" asked Ted, realising this was a new low, even for Franky.

"So, what? Wear them now, wear them next week, what's the difference?"

"I don't know, Franky, there's something not right... wearing a dead man's boots."

"How did you fall out with May, Franky?" asked Stacey.

Franky told the story of how rude May was, closing the door in his face when he asked her to say Jacky was driving when he got the speeding ticket.

This annoyed Ted. "No wonder she's not talking to you. I wouldn't either."

"Not talking to me? It's *me* who's not talking to her. She was just plain rude."

"It didn't stop you taking the boots though, did it?"

"No, it didn't. I didn't want to hurt her feelings. Her son had just died... I had to show a little respect."

Ted was glad to see the tea hut door opening and Martin appearing, not just because he was hungry but so that someone else could share the burden of Franky. Ted and Franky weren't long noticing that Martin was empty-handed.

"Did you not get the food, Martin?" asked Ted, curiously.

"Did you not get the food?" repeated Franky, not letting Martin answer the exact same question Ted had asked only a second before.

Martin told the story of the stupidity of the guy that worked in the café and how it came about that he had returned with no fries.

This gave Franky the perfect opportunity to whine on about the 'youth of today' again. "I told you, Ted. Didn't I tell you about that café boy? He's brain dead. They all are." Franky was disappointed about not getting any food but delighted at being proven right.

"Did you not watch him prepare the order?" asked Ted.

"No, I didn't. I suppose I should have been, in case any of those flaky bits came off his arms. Sorry da'."

"Why did you not replace the order and wait for it?" asked Franky.

"I didn't want to wait… tea break would've been over. I didn't care anyway, I got a bacon sandwich."

"Do the three of you want tea, anyway?" asked Stacey.

The three men agreed to have tea. As Stacey set Martin's tea in front of him, Franky was curious. "I thought you didn't like tea, Martin?"

"Will you read the leaves, Stacey?" asked Martin, with his puppy dog eyes.

Martin didn't like tea but what he did like was a laugh. He always got a laugh when he could get Stacey to read the tea leaves. Stacey, of course, couldn't read tea leaves. Can anybody? In Martin and Franky, she had a couple of gullible idiots who believed she could. But this morning, she wasn't in the mood.

"I don't do it anymore. You two know that," replied Stacey, insinuating that she used to, maybe professionally.

Martin continued, still with the puppy dog eyes. "Please, Stacey, for me."

Stacey relented. She reckoned if she read the leaves for them, it would stop them talking about Jacky. "OK, if it'll keep your minds off your bellies, I'll read them."

Franky was first. He took a sip of tea, threw out the rest and handed Stacey the cup.

"I can't read teabags, Franky."

"Sorry, Stacey."

Franky broke up the teabag in his cup and handed it back to Stacey.

Stacey put her mystic face on, and started reading. "I see sadness in this cup, Franky. Are you sad about anything?"

"Me? No. I've nothing to be sad about."

Martin, Stacey and Ted looked at Franky. Franky quickly realised that he should be sad at the passing of a 'friend'. He quickly changed his mind.

Stacey continued. "I see by the leaves that you have a sense of emptiness, Franky."

"Not really… hold on, my belly's empty. I never got any breakfast because of dick-weed here," answered Franky, giving Martin a dirty look.

"Wasn't my fault," Martin said, not caring at all that Franky missed his breakfast.

"How do you do it, Stacey? Those tea leaves are the business. You can tell I'm empty and sad, just by looking in that cup. How do you do it?"

"It's a gift, Franky."

Martin butted in. "It's my turn."

"Hold on, she's not finished with me yet. Anything else in there for me, Stacey?"

Stacey considered Franky's cup again. "Let me see… I see a dark stranger."

"Dark strangers are men. You're going to meet a dark stranger, and run away with him," declared Martin, intent on winding Franky up.

"Don't try to be funny, boy. I'm not gay. The dark stranger is a woman. Women can be dark too, you know."

"Is the stranger male or female?" asked Martin.

"Sorry, Franky, looks like the dark stranger is male," explained Stacey.

"I told you! You're a big homo," laughed Martin.

"It couldn't be. The stranger has to be female. Wait... I bet it's Ubeki," said Franky.

"Ubeki? Who's Ubeki?" asked Martin.

"He's a wee Ugandan kid I sponsor through UNICEF."

Martin was now very curious. "Sponsor? What do you mean, what's he doing?"

"What do you mean, what's he doing?" asked Franky, confused.

"What's he doing? A sky dive? A bungee jump? What are you sponsoring him for? Probably a half marathon or something, they're good at running."

"What are you talking about? Bungee jump? Sky dive? He lives in extreme poverty, Martin." Franky said.

"OK, what do you mean, you're sponsoring him?"

"They take a couple of quid a month out of my bank. They send me pictures of him. They keep me updated on his welfare. I have a picture here! Do you want to see it?"

Martin didn't want to see the picture. He reckoned it was pointless. "No, you're OK, I know what they look like."

"What the fuck does that mean? I know what *they* look like?" tested Franky.

"It doesn't mean anything. I'm just saying, I know what they look like," said Martin.

"You know what *who* looks like? Starving people? Poor people? Males? People called Ubeki? Maybe you're talking about black people? That's the most racist thing I've ever heard," sneered Franky.

"How is it racist? All I'm saying is, I see African kids on the TV all the time, and I know what they look like."

Franky turned to Ted for support. "Are you listening to this, Ted?"

Ted was back reading his paper and didn't look up from it. "Keep me out of this. It's between the pair of you, and all this tea leaves nonsense."

"They only have themselves to blame, if you ask me. I think they're just... bone idle," continued Martin.

"Bone idle? How do you make that out?" asked Franky, getting irritated at Martin's lack of sympathy.

"Whenever we see them on TV, there's always flies sitting on them. They couldn't even be bothered swiping the flies off their faces."

"Ted, are you listening to this? Are you listening to your son?" Ted ignored Franky and kept reading his paper.

"I see it all the time."

"Martin, did you know that when you don't eat, you have no energy? It's called *severe malnutrition*. You haven't the *energy* to scratch your balls. In most cases, especially the people they show on TV, they are close to death. Why would they use up what little energy they have worrying about a couple of *flies*?"

"Well, you never got your fry, and you've still energy to waffle on about Ukinky."

"Ubeki. His name is Ubeki, not Ukinky," Franky said. "Extreme malnutrition is a little different than missing your breakfast, do you not think?"

Ted, not listening to the conversation, decided to look up from his paper. "Franky, we'll chip in for a wreath. You go down at lunch time to get it."

"No problem, Ted. The three of us, chip in?"

"I hardly knew him," protested Martin.

"Don't be so miserable, you. I think fifteen pounds each would be enough."

"Fifteen pounds? What are you on, Franky? Are we paying for the coffin and all?"

"Don't try to be smart, Martin. I'll order a wreath in the shape of a tin of cider."

"Sure... was it not the cider that killed him?" quipped Martin.

Stacey, who was listening to everything, had a moment. Her heart sunk. In her paranoid head, she could have sworn that Martin said, "Was it not Stacey that killed him?" It was only when Franky answered Martin that she realised this wasn't what was said.

Franky continued. "It probably was. It's the thing he loved most though."

Martin thought this was hilarious. "Why not go the whole hog? Get a nice cirrhosis-rotted liver... framed. Stick it in his coffin."

"When big Tam gets his hands on you, we'll be putting a nice big toilet bowl in your coffin."

"Sure, it has to be something you like. How do I like toilet bowls?"

"You liked them enough earlier. Liked them enough to push big Tam out of the way to get onto one."

Ted had had enough of this inane conversation. "Martin, did bring your quilt covers and sheets into the laundry last night?"

"I did, da'."

"What's this? Still pissing the bed? How old are you now, boy?" jibed Franky.

"No, I wasn't pissing the bed!" protested Martin.

"Too much pulling at the old tool then? You not getting enough action?"

"I'm getting plenty of action. A lot more than you. They needed washing because there were paint stains on them."

"How did you get paint stains on your sheets?"

Ted answered. "Had the painters in on Saturday morning, painting his room."

"Did you not clear the bed sheets out of the room before they came?"

"No," answered Martin.

"Why not?"

"I was using them."

"What do you mean, you were using them?"

"I was in bed when they were decorating."

"What? Why didn't you get out of bed and let them do their job?"

"I was tired. It was also a bit annoying, that pair pushing me around when I was trying to sleep."

"Are you trying to tell me that they painted and papered your room, pushing you around in the bed while you slept?"

"What's wrong with that? Anyway, they didn't put the dust sheets over me properly. They got paint all over my quilt. Couple of cowboys if you ask me."

"They put a dust sheet over you?"

"What's wrong with that? You put dust sheets over TVs and stuff, it's the same thing. What's the difference?"

"What's the difference? The difference is that a TV hasn't got two legs to use to walk out of the room while they're trying to do their job."

"Could have been worse."

"How?"

"I could have had big Tam's knickers on when they were in."

Franky and Martin started laughing.

"If he knows you spilt the beans about those knickers, he'll strangle you with them," joked Franky, half serious.

"No chance. I would do big Tam," Martin retorted.

Franky never forgave Tam for telling everyone about his farting girlfriend. He took every chance to bring him down – everything except saying anything to his face.

"Do you know what happened to big Tam one time?" asked Franky.

"No, what happened?" Martin said, intrigued.

"He was working in New York on one of those skyscrapers… it was about twenty floors up, the winds were eighty miles an hour. He was walking across the twentieth floor up, carrying a sheet of plywood on his head, and the wind caught him and lifted him straight up into the air!"

"You're *kidding*! Was he killed?" Martin asked.

"What are you on? Did he not have his hands around your throat earlier? Of course, he wasn't killed! Did you hear what he just said there, Ted?"

"Leave me out of it," Ted mumbled.

Franky continued. "He flew straight off the top of the building, glided right down to the bottom, like a parachute. Landed on his feet."

"No *way*."

"Not only that, he carried the ply all the way up the stairs again… right up to the twentieth floor again."

"That's class! Are you serious?"

"Of course I'm not serious! Are *you* serious, believing that pile of shite?" Franky was now laughing at Martin's naivety.

"It could have happened, I don't know," Martin said.

"It could have happened? Who the fuck do you think he is? Spiderman?"

"He doesn't need to be Spiderman–"

Franky interrupted Martin. He looked out of the window and pretended Tam was coming into the hut. "There he is, big Tam. He's coming in."

Martin leapt up and jumped under the table.

Franky started laughing. "Thought you said you would do him?"

"That was before I heard about him flying off the skyscraper. He must have some strength in those arms."

"Stop lying! I told you, I made it up."

"If it didn't happen, something similar must have happened. You know the old saying… no smoke without a fryer."

"No smoke without a fryer? Where did you hear that one?"

"It's an old saying, Franky, don't tell me you've never heard it before?"

"Are you talking about, no smoke without fire? You really are thick. How could something similar have happened? I totally made it up."

"You must have gotten it from somewhere."

"I did, Martin. I got it from a mate of a mate whose cousin's wife's brother was on the job. He didn't see it, but they were all talking about it."

"Really?"

"*No*, Martin, not really. *I made it up*. Now give me the fifteen quid towards the wreath."

Ted handed Franky a five-pound note and a ten-pound note. "Here's mine, Franky."

"Thanks, Ted. Where's yours Martin?"

"I've no money on me. I'll give it to you tomorrow. Who's it for, anyway?"

"I told you earlier. Jacky Johnstone."

"When did he stop smoking?" Martin asked.

"What?" said Franky.

"Jacky Johnstone. When did he stop smoking?"

"Are you trying to be funny? Lost all respect for the dead now? Is that what the world's coming to?" Franky tested. "You die, you simply, stop smoking?"

"Listen, you. You weren't fit to lace Jacky's boots, so don't try to be clever."

Ted looked down at Franky's feet. "You are Franky, and you have the boots on to prove it."

Martin looked at Franky's feet. "Are those Jacky's boots?"

"And what?" Franky said.

"He was the same size as me! Did he have any raincoats? Winter's coming in."

"Have you no respect whatsoever? What are you asking me? Does he have any raincoats he won't be needing anymore?"

"Aye, did he?" Martin asked.

"Your stupidity… unbelievable."

"Why?"

"Do you not think, if he had any decent raincoats, I wouldn't have gotten them for myself?" Franky said.

"He was a labourer, wasn't he, Franky?"

"Yes, why?"

"Mate of mine's a labourer. He's looking for a start. Wherever Jacky was working will be a man short, won't they?"

Ted had heard enough. "Right, you two, that's enough. Stop talking like a pair of scavengers. Tea break's over, and remember your bonus."

"What bonus?" asked Martin.

"You work hard enough today, you'll have a job tomorrow." Ted said.

"Very funny, da', but Stacey hasn't read my tea leaves yet."

Ted turned to Stacey. "Have you a phone on you, Stacey?"

"Yes, Ted."

"Read Martin's tea leaves while we're away. Text him what they say, will you?"

"I will, Ted."

Franky couldn't help himself. "You'll not need tea leaves to read his future. It consists of a dirty big pair of hands with the name 'Tam' on them around his throat."

Ted called time on the tea break. Stacey started clearing the table as the three men left the hut. Four people with very different things on their minds.

Ted was worried about May. Ted himself had a son but had lost his wife. He had an idea of the pain she must be going through.

Martin, as he left the hut, was scouring the site for anyone who was willing to laugh at his revelation about Tam's underwear.

Franky was wondering how much he could get a wreath for and, if he could get it cheap enough, he may not have to put any money of his own into it.

Stacey was thinking about what would happen when they found out what Jacky's cause of death was. Would she be arrested?

CHAPTER SEVEN
THE TOILET DILEMMA

The Irish wake is a peculiar affair. Traditionally, the body lies in a family member's house, or their own home, for around three days and three nights. Friends and associates can then call at any time during this seventy-two hour period, day or night, to see the corpse. I say corpse because that's exactly what it is. Visitors would place a mass card, purchased from a local shop, in the occupied coffin and say a prayer. The body, before being placed on show, is embalmed to avoid decomposition. This is very important as the body would start to rot before the very eyes of the family. The typical fluid used is formaldehyde. The three main reasons for this process are sanitisation, presentation and preservation.

'Need to call to this wake to show my face' is the declaration, in private, of most of the people who go to them. Of course, this type of guest to the wake doesn't realise that the nearest and dearest of the deceased (who are so engrossed in their grief) cares not who is there and who is not. One of the most ridiculous comments commonly said as the guest looks into the coffin is that the occupant is looking 'well' – something they would never had said while the deceased was still alive.

Jacky's wake was different to most others. For various reasons, he was only to be waked for one day and one night. He died on the Sunday but, because of the bank holiday Monday, his body wasn't brought to May's house until Tuesday. The priest couldn't perform the funeral mass on the Thursday or Friday, so May had no choice other than to bury him on the Wednesday.

Another thing about the Irish wake is that there is always a lot of alcohol involved. After the funeral, most of the friends and family would return from the graveyard and go to a local pub where the deceased family would be forced, through tradition, to lay on a buffet to feed the so-called mourners. May said she wasn't laying any such thing on after the burial. She had seen her son's deterioration through drink and didn't want to entice anyone into drinking alcohol.

For some reason, maybe because of May not having a funeral do, everyone got together on the Tuesday evening to celebrate Jacky's life. Some had already been in to see Jacky but others just headed straight to the bar without even bothering to 'show their face'. The local bar was packed for a Tuesday. Landlords love funeral parties. All the worst business days of their week – Monday, Tuesday, Wednesday and Thursday – can see the bar packed out if they are the hosts of a funeral party.

Stacey worked part-time at this local bar. She decided to work the Tuesday and take the Wednesday off. She didn't realise that the funeral crowd would be in on the Tuesday because of May's refusal to have a funeral party on Wednesday, the day of the burial.

Martin was enjoying the craic at the party. After a few pints, he ventured to the toilet. As he entered, he could see Franky standing alone. He was talking to himself. Martin didn't know what he was mumbling, nor did he care.

"*Boo!*" shouted Martin, right into Franky's ear, who was unaware that Martin had entered the toilet.

"Fuck ye! You scared the shit out of me there," barked Franky, rubbing the ear Martin shouted into.

"What are you doing here?" asked Martin, still laughing at making Franky jump.

"Am I not allowed to go to the toilet now?"

"But you're not going to the toilet. You're standing there talking to yourself."

"Am I not allowed to stand here now? Last I checked, it was a free country."

"It's only perverts and homos who loiter in toilets. Which are you – a pervert or a homo?"

"Watch your mouth, boy. I'm neither."

"What are you doing here, then?"

"It's got nothing to do with you, Martin. Do your business, then go."

As the two men bickered, the door opened and in walked a black man – a handsome, tall black man, impeccably dressed, in his mid- to late-forties. He totally ignored Martin and Franky, walking straight over to the mirror. When he got to the mirror, he started to rub his wrists.

Martin greeted him. "How's it going, The King?"

The King answered without taking his eyes of the mirror. "Everything's cool for cats, son. Cool for cats. What about yourself?"

"I'm dead on, The King, thanks for asking. What's that on your shirt?"

"My fake tan started to run a bit, just wiping it off my shirt."

On hearing this, Franky (being Franky) couldn't hold it in. "Fake tan? What the fuck are you wearing fake tan for? You're black."

"My skin gets a bit blotchy. What's it got to do with you, anyway, clown?" The King was still focused on the mirror. He still didn't look around at the two men.

"I'm no clown, son. I think it's an obvious question. Who are you anyway?"

"That's The King, Franky," declared Martin.

"The what?"

"The King."

"The King of what? The King of where?"

The King walked over and opened a cubical door. "Right, I'm going to have a shit now, keep the noise down." The King closed the cubical door behind him.

Franky was a bit perplexed. "Who the fuck's that joker? Why do you call him The King? Why does he need it to be quiet to shit?"

Franky did notice the colour of The King's skin. There wasn't a racist bone in his body. Franky was old school – he would use all the words that offended black people but wouldn't know they were offensive words. A lot of the older generation of Belfast were like this. In conversation where a black person was mentioned, the most common word they would use is darkie. They would use it, but wouldn't mean to offend in any way.

****

In Belfast in the sixties and seventies, it would be rare to see anyone other than Caucasians on the streets. People, no matter what colour they were, were not going to move to war-torn Belfast. There was sectarianism but no racism, simply because there was no one to be racist to. Incidentally, The Heath government of the early seventies had a solution to the 'Irish problem'. They had no idea how to stop the factions, and Catholics and Protestants murdering each other daily. They reckoned that re-housing black and Asian people in Belfast would stop the sectarianism and, eventually, the natives would turn on the minorities. This silly idea was probably concocted in an upper crust gentleman's club, where politicians with no common sense thought that racism and hatred was better than sectarianism and hatred. Of course, the results would have been that the minorities would have been set upon if the Catholics couldn't get their hands on a Protestant or vice versa. Hopefully this idea was never motioned at the cabinet table in Downing Street. Or maybe it was. Who knows?

****

"I've no idea why he's called The King. I asked him his name earlier. He said to call him The King, so I did," Martin explained to Franky.

"You must be kidding? He told you to call him The King, and you just started calling him it?"

"What would you like me to call him? If he said that's his name, then that's his name."

"I don't know, there's something weird about asking people to call you The King. Not even King but: The King?"

"Give the guy a break, Franky. Someone was telling me earlier that he gave his girlfriend the money for a boob job a few years ago, and she left him as soon as she got them."

"What? Some other guy's playing with the knockers he paid for?"

The King could hear the men talking from the other side of the cubicle. "She didn't leave me. I cut her loose."

Franky was still finding it hard to come to terms with someone calling themselves 'The King'. "I suppose she was called 'The Queen'?" Franky said, loud enough for The King to know he was talking to him.

"No, her name was Karen."

"Why wasn't she called The Queen, if you're The King?"

"We weren't married."

"Sorry, my mistake," Franky retorted sarcastically, rolling his eyes.

"What did you ditch her for, The King?" asked Martin.

"She had a bad attitude, or should I say, an ungrateful attitude."

"What do you mean?" queried Martin.

"It was the sex. She never once thanked me... not once."

The fact that someone called himself 'The King' was really getting on Franky's nerves. "That is ridiculous! You can't expect a girl to thank you after sex. Why would she?"

"I wanted thanking during sex, not after it. Why wouldn't they thank me? I'm The King."

"You're The King of Bullshit, if you ask me."

The King decided he had had enough conversation with Franky. "OK, no more talking, I'm busy here."

Martin remembered he was in the toilet for a reason. He entered the second cubicle and closed the door behind him. Just as Martin locked the cubicle door, a fourth person entered the toilet: Cecil.

Cecil, whose flat Franky had broken into (and in which Franky had found the child molestation court depositions), still owed Franky that money. He was also the boy who Franky claims to have molested him all those years ago. Franky had seen him earlier in the bar, which led him to go to the toilet in the first place to get some quiet, so he could figure out how to approach him. He had no choice now. He was in front of him; he had to confront him.

"All right, Franky?" Cecil said pleasantly, as he started to unzip at the urinal.

Franky wasn't pleased at the sheer cheek of Cecil. "Listen here, Cecil, don't talk to me like we have some kind of friendship. We're not friends. I have real friends in here."

"I'm not his friend," The King declared from behind his cubicle door.

"Do you mind?" replied Franky. "This is a private conversation. I wasn't talking about you, anyway, I was talking about him." Franky pointed to the other cubicle door.

Cecil had a creepy nature about him. Always pleasant and never got riled. He would look you up and down. You would just know the thoughts he was thinking weren't nice. As he rolled his eyes up and down your body, inspecting you, you knew his thoughts were either of distain or perversion. He had fair hair, was dressed well and handsome enough to give himself all the confidence he needed. "Long time no see, Franky. How have you been keeping?"

"What a brass neck. You have a cheek to show your face around here, after what you did," Franky said.

"I didn't do anything. I was found not guilty of all charges. They were all dropped."

"What are you talking about?"

"The kid. She was lying."

"I'm not talking about that. Why would I care about that? I'm taking about the money you owe me."

"Oh, that… for the job? Sorry, Franky, things were a bit tight then. I'll give you your money. I've money here… how much do I owe you?"

"Five hundred quid."

Cecil pulled out a wad of notes – far more than five hundred.

Franky immediately saw Cecil was carrying big dough and, of course, he got greedy. "And a little compensation on top of the five hundred?"

"Compensation? For what?"

"For that time you molested me."

"Molested you? I never molested you."

"Yes, you did," Franky argued. "You got me at the derelict houses one time, stripped me down to my Y-fronts, treated me like a slave all fucking day."

"I don't think that qualifies as molestation, Franky. We were just having a laugh."

"A laugh? I was traumatised… couldn't sleep for months. I still have nightmares."

"You loved it! Master this, master that… you asked if you could come back the next day."

"I did not ask to go back the next day, fucking pervert."

"I'm one year older than you, Franky, how could I molest you?"

"You were far bigger."

"Has to be at least five years older to be molestation," shouted The King, still in the cubical.

"How the fuck would you know?" Franky asked The King angrily.

"Because I am The King."

"The King of Balls. Mind your own business."

Franky realised that seeking compensation for bullying dressed as molestation wasn't going to cut it – not in this case. He turned his attention back on the five hundred he was owed.

"OK, I'll wave the compensation on the technicality that you were only a year older. I still want that five hundred."

"OK, you can have the five hundred on one condition."

"What condition?"

"You give me a big hug. A big, squashy hug! Let bygones be bygones."

"Fuck off, I'm not hugging you, you pervert."

"No hugs, no chugs."

"What's chugs?"

"Money."

"No, it's not. You just made that up because it rhymes with hugs."

"Franky, if you want the five hundred, I want a forgive-and-forget hug."

"What about a handshake?"

"I want a hug."

Franky wanted the five hundred; it was within arm's reach. He didn't want to mess it up now.

"OK, a hug it is then."

"I knew you'd see sense! Come here."

Just as Cecil moved towards Franky with outstretched arms, he slipped on the wet floor, cracking his head against the tiled step. Within a few seconds, Cecil was lying on the ground motionless. As Franky stared at the unconscious Cecil in disbelief, Martin stepped out of the cubicle.

"Jesus, Franky! Did you kill him?"

"I never laid a finger on him."

"You cracked him. He was going to tell everyone you gave him a blow job."

"What blow job?"

"He said he gave you a blow job."

"He did *not*."

"I heard him."

"I heard him say it, too," interjected The King, now out of his cubical. "He gave you a blow job."

"A job. He said he gave me a *job*."

"Doesn't really matter now, he's dead." said Martin, casually.

Franky started to panic. He kneeled down next to Cecil, looking for a pulse. "He's not dead."

Martin tried to console Franky. "Could be worse, Franky."

"How could it be worse? I think the fucker's dead... it can't get much worse."

"I think Cecil's an old pervert. You'll not spend as much time in gaol, killing one of them, as you would if you had killed a normal person."

"What are you talking about?" Franky said. "It'll be far worse – hate crime and all that. I'm doing no time anyway, I never touched him. Where's his pulse? How do I check for a pulse?"

"I don't know, on his arm or something. Give him the kiss of life."

"I'm not giving that thing the kiss of life! You do it, Martin."

"I'm not going near him. You do it."

"Go on, Martin, please. Just a wee kiss of life."

"You do it. It was all right when you took the blow job off him but now there's an audience, you don't want to know."

As the two men bickered, The King stepped over the body on the ground without even looking at it, and proceeded to wash his hands. "You would think," announced The King, "with six bar staff working, they would send one into the toilet now and again, to clean it. The place is a mess."

Franky looked at The King, amazed that he had totally ignored the body on the floor and was more worried about the cleanliness of the toilets. "Not up to your highness's high standards? Is it not as sanitised as his majesty's palace?"

Martin turned to The King. "The King, what are we going to do about the dead guy on the floor?"

"There's an old Nigerian saying... if someone puts a big pile of shite at your door, you must clean that shite yourself. No one is going to clean it for you." The King left the toilet, saying nothing else.

"I think that one was lost in translation. Great fucking help he was," yapped Franky.

"What are you going to do here, Franky? My pint'll be warm when I get back to it."

"You can put ice in it."

"It's not the same with ice... it ruins it."

Before the two men could argue further about whether a pint of beer loses quality if ice is placed in it, the toilet door opened again. A young barman walked in with a mop and bucket. He walked past the body on the ground and started to mop the cubicle that The King frequented moments earlier.

Franky stared in disbelief, this time at the young barman who totally ignored the body on the ground. "Barman, can you not see? There's a body on the floor."

"Where?"

"Where? *Where*? This fucking body! The one you nearly tripped over." Franky pointed to Cecil.

"What about it?"

"Would you please do something? He could be dead."

"But, The King said..."

"Fuck The King," Franky interrupted. "Phone someone. There's a body lying here, and we don't know if it's alive or dead."

The young barman was at a loss and didn't know what to do. He took out his phone and started flicking through his numbers. He finally admitted that he had no idea who to phone. "Who will I Google? The undertakers? A funeral parlour? Or are they the same thing?"

"Why would you be phoning an undertaker?" asked Franky.

"He's dead, isn't he?"

"We don't know if he's dead."

"Who should I phone then?"

"Who do you *usually* phone… a doctor, an ambulance?"

Martin spotted the brand-new device the barman was holding. "Is that the new iPhone?"

"Yeah," answered the barman. "Brilliant, aren't they? Thirty-five pounds per month!"

Franky snapped. "Never mind the *fucking* iPhone, just ring someone."

The young barman eventually called a number. "Hello, is that dial-a-cab?"

"What are you *doing*?" Franky asked the barman.

"What are you doing, ringing those robbing bastards?" chirped Martin, genuinely shocked that anyone would phone such an expensive taxi place.

Franky asked again. "Why are you phoning a taxi?"

"Who would you like me to phone?"

"A doctor! Just phone a fucking doctor! Quick."

"There's a doctor out in the bar."

"What? In this bar?"

"Yes, he's sitting out there," pointed the barman.

"Go *fucking* get him then."

The barman scampered off to get the doctor.

"I wonder if I should get one of those iPhones. They look all right," Martin said to Franky.

"Would you give over about iPhones," Franky said, irritated. "There's a guy on the floor… could be dead… and all you can talk about is iPhones."

Franky and Martin were left hovering over Cecil's body for about a minute, then the door opened and in walked the young barman with The King.

Franky was confused. "Where's the doctor?"

The barman pointed to The King. "There he is."

"*You* are the doctor? Why didn't you say?"

"What do you do for a living?" The King asked Franky.

"I'm a builder."

"Why didn't you say?"

"You were here five minutes ago! Why didn't you look at him then?"

"My pints were getting warm."

"Your pints were getting warm? Are you serious?"

Martin interrupted. "He says to put ice in them, but they're not the same when you put ice in them, are they, The King?"

The King, it seemed, had the same opinion as Martin when it came to putting ice in beer. "Not the same. May as well throw them out."

"Would you shut up about iPhones and warm beer! Is he OK?" Franky questioned.

The King puts his hands on Cecil's head, mumbled a few words, and Cecil's eyes started to open.

"What happened?" asked Cecil, still dazed.

"You had a little accident." answered The King.

Cecil started to feel the arse of his trousers.

"Not that kind of accident," explained The King. "You slipped and banged your head."

Franky jumped in. "You were just about to give me five hundred pound... the money you owe me."

"Pull the other one, I think I would remember something like that," Cecil replied.

"But..." Franky tried to plead his case but was ignored.

Cecil was a bit shaken but left the toilets with the barman unaided. Franky let the small detail of the five hundred go for now. He was just relieved that he wasn't being charged with some sort of hate crime. As The King went to leave, Franky wanted to show his gratitude – in words, not currency.

"Thank you, doctor," Franky said.

The King ignored Franky and left the toilet. Franky was still miffed at The King's arrogance.

"Did you see that, Martin?"

"What?"

"I thanked him, and he didn't even acknowledge me. Just rudeness."

"He probably didn't know you were talking to him," Martin said.

"Why?"

"You called him 'doctor' – his name is The King!"

"For fuck's sake... stop saying that name."

After the altercation, the men left the toilet and went to their respective seats. The King sat alone, close to the bar. Although it was a big enough bar, Franky couldn't believe he hadn't noticed him earlier. Simply because he was the only black man in the place, he thought he should have clocked him. After scanning the place for him, Franky spotted where The King was sitting. Curious as to who this person was and why he was here, he made his way over to him.

The King had been watching everyone all night – without, of course, anyone knowing they were being watched. He was now watching Franky approach. As he approached, Franky spotted a twenty-pound note. It was lying right at the feet of The King. He couldn't lift it and put it in his pocket; The King would almost certainly see him. He decided… it was the perfect introduction.

"Is this yours?" asked Franky, picking up the twenty-pound note and showing it to The King.

"Yes," answered The King, taking the twenty-pound note without hesitation and without even checking his wallet.

"How do you know? How do you know it's yours without checking your pockets to see if you lost it?"

"I dropped it earlier."

"Then why didn't you pick it up?"

"Why should I? I knew some wanker would come along and pick it up for me."

"Wanker? Are you calling me a wanker? It's only a wanker that calls himself The King."

"Are you still here?" asked The King sarcastically, without even looking at Franky.

Before Franky could rant, Martin interrupted. "Well, how's The King?" he asked. Martin liked The King. He had good intuition.

"I'm OK, kid." answered The King, again without looking at him.

"Hey, The King, I came across a group on YouTube the other day – Boney M, I think they were called, from the seventies – did you ever hear of them?"

"Why are you asking me? Because I'm black?"

"No, because you look like you may have been knocking about in the seventies."

"What about them? They were shit."

"I don't know if they were, The King. I think they were discos political thinkers, way ahead of their time."

This tickled The King. He started laughing at Martin. "Discos political thinkers? What the fuck are you talking about boy?"

"Belfast, Ma Baker, Rasputin… they were tuned into the times. Makes you think."

"Makes you think? Tuned into the times? It makes you think all right – it makes you think of how sad the seventies were, allowing that bunch of fucking clowns on TV."

"You might be wrong there, The King. They were actually singing serious songs about history."

"Serious songs? Are you on drugs, son? They had a song out called Bang Bang Lulu. What the fuck is serious about that? Unless you banged Lulu and she gave you the clap. Then it would be very serious."

Franky was now starting to sense that there was an importance about this man. He may not be a King but there was something about him… he couldn't put his finger on it. Franky decided that, although The King's arrogance irked him, it would be more beneficial if he befriended him.

"These young lads… they haven't a clue, King. Morons, the lot of them."

"*The* King," corrected The King.

"Sorry, The King." By this time, Franky had pulled up a seat beside The King, who wasn't looking too pleased.

"I was saying, these young lads…" Franky continued.

"Who invited you to sit down?" The King asked Franky, this time looking at him.

Franky ignored The King's reaction to him sitting down beside him. "I've been inquiring about you," said Franky, cockily. "You're no doctor. You're a grave digger."

"Investigate and inquire all you like. Just do it somewhere else," responded The King.

"What did you do to Cecil? How did you mend him?"

"He mended himself."

"You mumbled something into his ear, then he responded and came around. What did you say to him?"

"Don't interfere with things you know nothing about."

"What?" asked Franky. "What do I know nothing about?"

The King turned to Franky. He stared him right in the eyes. "The dark side."

These words and the sombre way they were said had creeped Franky out. He was uneasy. The three men sat in silence for a few minutes. Franky didn't want to leave the company yet. He thought that knowing or being friends with The King would be to his advantage. The dark side stuff had creeped him out, so he decided to change the subject. Franky thought, for some reason, now would be a good time to throw out some of his stand-up material.

"Those Bee Gees brothers… they sang a song called Too Much Heaven. That's exactly what they're getting now."

There was no response or laughter from Martin or The King.

"I wonder," Franky continued, "did those brothers die of a fever on a Saturday night?"

Still nothing. Not a smirk from Martin or The King.

Franky still continued. "And that other song… Staying Alive… who let them write that? That's something they shouldn't be writing about. It's something they don't have a clue about… Staying Alive."

Still no laughter.

The King was getting bored with Franky, so he decided to play with him. "I have a job for you, Franky." said The King, earnestly.

"I don't need a job. I have a job." answered Franky.

"It's double the money you're getting now."

"How do you know what I'm getting now?"

"I don't know. I heard you were a great worker. Whatever you're on now, I'll double it."

Now we're getting to it, Franky thought. This boy has a few quid. Franky wanted his taste. "Do you want me to dig graves? Dig graves for double the money I'm on now? I'm interested."

"The job isn't digging graves."

"Not digging graves? What is it then?"

"It's down at the beach. You can start in the morning."

"Start in the morning? I can't… it's Jacky's funeral in the morning."

"Start on Thursday then."

"OK, no problem. What will I be doing at the beach?"

"Putting sand into skips."

"Sand? For the builder's yard? Sounds great, I'll be there. Are you sure it's double the money?"

"Yes."

"I'll be there."

"Just one thing, Franky."

"What's that?"

"Bring your own spoon."

Martin and The King burst into laughter. Franky was furious. He'd had enough of this person. He stood up to leave the company but The King had one more thing to say to him. For only the second time that evening, The King looked into Franky's eyes.

"I know what you did to Jacky."

Franky was taken aback with this comment. "What are you talking about?"

"You *know* what I'm talking about," replied The King.

Franky knew better than to inquire more about what The King knew. He was slightly worried but not enough to stop him getting the last word in.

"Don't start your voodoo shit with me," Franky said, before storming off.

Stacey, having chosen to work that night instead of the following day, was behind the bar. Still wrecked with worry and guilt, she decided to keep her head down and keep busy. Better working in any case, she thought. God knows what she would say if she was here drinking.

As Franky left the bar area, The King decided he needed a drink. He had been eying Stacey most of the night. He knew her but she didn't know him. He approached the bar. Stacey was waiting to serve him.

Stacey's thoughts deviated from Jacky for just a moment. She was curious as to who the handsome stranger was. She thought she knew him but just couldn't put her finger on it. She decided to ask.

"Did you know Jacky?" she asked, setting a pint on the counter.

"Oh, I knew Jacky. We were the best of friends years back."

"Oh yeah? What's your name?"

"The King."

"*You're* The King? Jacky used to mention you all the time. About when you two used to dig graves."

"That would be me. I hope it was all good."

"He never mentioned you were black, though."

"Why would he?"

"Right enough… why would he, indeed."

"How much is that?" The King asked, pointing to his pint.

"This one's on me." replied Stacey. "Jacky told me grave digging with you were the best days of his life."

"They would have been, but he did fuck all work for a lot of money," replied The King, jokingly.

"They were good days, Stacey. It's a pity the drink got a hold of him."

"It's a pity. He was truly happy then."

"There's no such thing as being truly happy, Stacey."

"Why's that?"

"We can never be truly happy because it will all end someday. No matter how happy you are, you're still going to die in the end."

"Some people aren't afraid of dying, you know."

"Very few of us are afraid to die… we would just rather be alive than dead."

"How did you know my name? How did you know I went out with Jacky?"

"I just did, Stacey. I know a lot."

Stacey didn't think much of this comment. She had heard a lot of bullshit in the bar. She had a smile on her face as The King walked away from the bar with his pint. The smile wasn't for The King; the smile was for Jacky and for the days he was happy.

Stacey's smile quickly disappeared though. Halfway between The King's seat and the bar, he stopped walking. Stacey was still looking at him. He turned around, looked directly into Stacey's eyes and, loud enough for only her to hear, he spoke five words.

"*I know what you did.*"

He then turned his back on her and returned to his seat. The King sat down and didn't look at Stacey again.

Stacey, already a paranoid wreck, was speechless. Her gut wrenched and she started shaking. How could he know anything about what happened to Jacky? He must be talking about something else. Did Jacky tell him about that Sunday when she slept with three people? No, Jacky would never talk about her. Jacky wouldn't even confide something like that to The King. He would know how embarrassing it would be for her. What was he on about? *I know what you did*? Stacey was left to stew on these words for the rest of the night. As if she wasn't bad enough before, she was now approaching a breakdown.

As Franky sat alone at the other side of the bar, the words that The King had uttered, with that evil look, had begun to sink in. He was thinking much the same as Stacey. How could The King know? Is he an African witch doctor? Does he do that black magic shit? How did he know he was at Jacky's the night he died? Maybe he was talking about something else? He mentioned Jacky's name… or did he? Franky was worried and confused. He calmed himself. The King was obviously talking about Cecil and what happened in the toilet. Now that Franky was calm he started to think about the twenty-pound note he found. Was it The King's? If only he'd have gone to the table when The King was at the bar or toilet. He would have been twenty pounds richer. This – more than Jacky's death, Cecil's close shave or The King belittling him – annoyed him the most for the rest of the evening.

****

While these exchanges between Franky, The King and Stacey were going on in the bar, there was someone hovering about watching the situation unravel. Big Tam. He had seen The King leave the bar and had observed Stacey getting upset. He wasn't nosy, but he did look after his friends, so he approached Stacey, who was still shaken.

"Are you OK, Stacey?"

"I'm OK, Tam. Why? Has someone said something?" replied Stacey. Paranoia was creeping in at Tam's questioning.

"No," replied Tam. "No one's said anything. I thought that dark fella had said something rude to you. Do you know him?"

"Yes, I know him… well, I don't *know* him. I've heard of him… he was a friend of Jacky's."

"A friend of Jacky's, was he? It didn't look like he was saying hello. You looked upset when he left."

"He was talking about Jacky and the old days. I just got a bit emotional, that's all."

Tam wasn't convinced by Stacey's story. He looked over at The King, The King was staring at him. Tam couldn't let it go, so he approached him.

"Do I know you?" asked Tam.

"Maybe you do, maybe you don't. We all look the same to you people," replied The King, sarcastically.

"That's not what I meant. I was wondering why you were staring at me?"

The King didn't beat about the bush this time. He stared right into Tam's eyes and spoke those same words. "I know what you did."

You could have knocked big Tam down with a feather. "What? What did I do?"

The King looked away from Tam. He didn't answer him.

Tam persisted. "What are you talking about? What did I do?"

The King ignored him.

"Answer the fucking question. What did I do?'

Again, The King refused to acknowledge Tam. Tam was getting angry now; he was going into the zone – the zone where he's so angry, he doesn't know what he's doing. But he managed to pull back, just before the fireworks. Tam walked away from The King, uneasy, unsettled. Unlike Franky and Stacey, Tam knew that The King knew something about what happened that night. But what?

Tam went home. He thought he knew this guy's face. It irritated him. He'd seen him before. But where? He just couldn't put his finger on it. He couldn't remember that it was the black guy sitting in the BMW outside Jacky's house. The night they left Jacky's house. The night Jacky died.

CHAPTER EIGHT
THE NIGHT RIDER

Earlier that Tuesday, Tam had waited on Martin coming back from the café. After they had words, Tam wasn't seen in work the rest of the day. Tam was worried about May. To be honest, Tam's own predicament as to what happened in Jacky's house the night he died didn't mean a lot to him. He was honestly and genuinely worried about May. He took the day off to call to her house to see if she needed anything.

To most people who Jacky knew, he was just another alcoholic who abused himself to the point of destruction. Tam, however, knew what Jacky meant to May. If anyone in the world knew, it was Tam. Every day from the time May spoke to him down the alley when he was a boy, Tam kept an eye on her. This was her hour of need, Tam thought. She would need him now more than ever.

May was sat alone at home that morning. She was sipping tea when she heard a slight tap on the hall door. He didn't even wait until she answered the door – there he was, standing in her living room, the undertaker. Bart the bastard. His hooked nose, receding hairline, gaunt face and long chin were all on show. Not the kind of person to lift your spirits. He immediately gave his condolences, but this didn't last long.

"Mrs Johnstone, how are you holding up? It's a sad, sad occasion."

May was taken aback by this depressing figure standing in her living room. She quickly remembered him from the hospital. Bartholomew Butt.

"I'm holding up well, Mr Butt."

Without invitation, the undertaker, sat himself down on the sofa. It was hard sell time. "Your only son, Mrs Johnstone. He'll be coming home to you soon and I'm sure you'll be looking to give him a good send off."

"I haven't got much money, Mr Butt."

"Good gracious me, Mrs Johnstone. We don't think about money at times like this. We'll just decide on the casket, fitting for an only son. We'll settle up after the funeral."

"Something simple, I think."

"I have the Diamond Blue coffin. Comes in at around two thousand. It's one of our most popular. It would usually retail at around four thousand, but we're doing an offer on it at the minute."

"I can't afford it."

"Don't be worrying about that, Mrs Johnstone. We have a very affordable payment plan."

"I don't want any debt, Mr Butt. Thank you for the offer, but I'll just go with the basic. Thank you."

"Basic? For your only son? Wouldn't be fitting, Mrs Johnstone! Remember, you only die once. Let me just see what the repayments will be."

Butt inappropriately took out his calculator to work out a payment plan. May wasn't fizzed at this intruder. Her mind was enveloped by only one thing: her dead son.

As Butt started to throw out numbers, the door knocked again. This person didn't wait on May answering either. He popped his head around the door, but this person was allowed to walk on in. It was Tam.

"Are you home, May?"

"I am, son. Come on in."

Tam entered the living room and immediately saw Butt sitting on the settee. Tam had no idea who Butt was, and immediately assumed he was a friend of May's.

"Sorry, May. I didn't know you had company, I'll call back later."

"Not at all, son. Come in, sit down."

It only took a few minutes of Tam sitting in the same room as Butt for him to realise what an awful person he was looking at. The vulgarity of him, talking money, offers, once-in-a-lifetime deals. Tam quickly grew angry with this man. May must have invited him into her home, he thought, so he had to hold his tongue. Tam also had a sense that he knew Butt. That niggling feeling in the back of his mind. He knew he knew him, but couldn't put his finger on it. Much the same as with The King. He knew the face but couldn't quite remember why. It was probably the years of alcohol abuse that didn't serve Tam's memory too well.

Butt continued, unperturbed that Tam was there. "I've done my calculations, Mrs Johnstone. If we take the payment plan over four years…"

"I really can't afford it," pleaded May.

"As I say, he was your only son. Surely you don't want your only son buried in a cardboard coffin?"

Tam tried to remain polite, but for what little conversation he had heard, he'd heard enough. "Are those ears painted on?" asked Tam, turning to Butt, not an inkling of a smile.

"Whatever do you mean?"

"I'll tell you what I mean. Your ears must be painted on because you don't seem to hear what she's saying. She doesn't want a big fancy coffin. She's a pensioner on a pension. She can't afford it."

Butt realised he had no chance of bullying May any further while Tam was there. She wasn't buying the Diamond Blue. May would have loved to buy her son the most expensive one if she had the money, Jacky would have got a horse drawn carriage, Westminster cathedral, the works. She simply couldn't afford it, and she never got into debt.

Butt had another suggestion. "Have you ever thought of cremation, Mrs Johnstone?"

"Oh, no, my boy's not getting cremated."

"Before you reject it, we're doing a relatively new thing. After cremation, we gather some of the ashes, put them in small bags with a picture of your son, and then sell them afterwards. His friends and family buy them as a keepsake. We sell the bags for twenty pounds each – you get ten pounds, we get ten pounds. If we sell, let's say, twenty bags, then you have two hundred pounds towards the funeral costs."

Tam was so astounded by this proposition that he briefly thought about lifting Bart up by the face and throwing him clean through the window out into the street. But he was curious.

"Who sells these bags of ashes?"

"We leave them in the bar, or we can take orders when they are leaving the crematorium. We'll need a ten-pound deposit for orders."

"Why don't you just get a vending machine for them?" asked Tam, sarcastically.

"A vending machine? Goodness gracious, no, how crude would that be?"

"How crude would that be? About as crude as asking an old lady to fry up her son, bag him up, and punt out the contents. Have you no scruples whatsoever?"

"There's no need for aggression. I'm just proposing options to help Mrs Johnstone with the funeral costs… that's all I'm doing."

"May's friends and family will help out with the costs. We'll not need a bag of her dead son to do that, either. What I would like to do right now is set fire to your hair, and put the flames out with my fists. I'd then bag your ashes. I wouldn't sell them though, because no one would buy them. I'd feed them to the pigs."

May sensed that Tam was on attack mode. She tried to defuse the situation. "Tam, would you make me a cup of tea, son?"

Tam looked at May, then looked at Bart. He didn't want to leave her alone with him, but he always did what she told him. "OK, May. Give me a wee shout if you need me."

Tam got up out of the chair and went to the kitchen. After making the tea and not offering the undertaker any, he returned to the living room, two cups of tea in hand. Butt had gone. May was sat in tears.

"Don't worry about it, May. You can get Jacky any coffin you like. We'll sort it out somehow. I'll get all the boys to chip in," Tam said softly, as he sat next to her on the settee.

"I'm not crying over the coffin, son. Pay no heed, I'm just a silly old woman."

"What did he say? Did that creepy fucker say something to you when I was making the tea? I'll choke that fucker."

Tam jumped up off the settee and headed for the door. He wanted to catch hold of Butt before he slithered too far away.

"Sit down, Tam, sit down."

Tam, of course, did what he was told. He lifted May's tea and put it in her hand. May's tears had now stopped. She was drying her eyes with a paper handkerchief.

Tam wasn't convinced. "What happened May? What did he do? You were fine when I left to make the tea. I come back, you're in tears, and he's gone. He must have done something."

"Just leave it, Tam, it doesn't matter."

"May, I promise you this… if you don't tell me, I'll go around to that undertaker and I'll beat it out of him."

"It's personal, just leave it."

"If you're in tears, it's not personal anymore. It becomes my business."

"I'll tell you. You must promise never to tell anyone. Do you promise, Tam?"

"Of course. I promise, May. I'll take it to the grave, you know that."

"Our Jacky, he had a lovely head of hair, hadn't he?"

"It was nice, I never paid much attention. Looked OK to me."

"It was a toupee."

"A wig?"

"No, a toupee. He was bald at the front. He started going bald when he was sixteen. He got terribly depressed over it, so I got him a toupee. He wore it all his life, and it never left his head… through all his sickness, his drunken escapades, he kept it on."

"Is that right? Fair play to him. He did a great job. None of his mates knew anything about it. What's that got to do with the undertaker, though?"

"Oh, Tam. I'm so frightened that the toupee will come off when he's in the coffin, what with people touching him, kissing him, and the like."

"It'll hardly matter now, May, he's dead. I can't see him worrying too much."

May threw Tam a dirty look.

Tam received it, loud and clear. "Sorry, May, I know what you mean. It's his dignity. Of course it still matters." Tam regretted being so coarse. He, however, knew all about Jacky's dignity. His dignity when he soiled himself, or his dignity the numerous times he pissed himself, or his dignity all the times he was borrowing money for drink. Tam knew, possibly from his own personal experience, that dignity is a luxury when it comes to people who are dependent on drugs or alcohol. Dignity is the first thing you trade in when falling for those types of addiction. As far as May was concerned, he was a good boy, so Tam wasn't going to tell her any different.

"What's Jacky being bald got to do with the undertaker, May?"

"I told him, no matter what, I didn't want the toupee coming off his head when he's in the coffin... oh, Tam..."

The thoughts of the conversation with Bart the bastard set May off sobbing again.

"What did he say?" asked Tam.

"He said, don't worry about it, a couple of nails don't cost much."

"He said *what*?"

"My poor boy... he's going to nail his toupee to his head. Tam, what am I going to do?"

"Did you tell him? Did you tell him not to nail it to his head?"

"I didn't get a chance. I started crying and before I knew it, he was gone."

"Don't worry about it. I'll go and see him. You've enough on your plate without having to worry about this."

"Will you tell him, Tam? Tell him he can't do that to my son, and don't cause a fuss, please."

"No problem, I'll sort it."

"Thank you, son."

"No problem, May, leave it with me."

May was trying to hold in her tears, but couldn't.

"It's killing me, son, I don't want to let him go. Do you not think he could stay here with me in the spare room?"

"When he comes home? Until he gets buried?"

"No, Tam, for good. Until I die?"

"May, that's not possible, you know that. You don't need me to tell you what happens to a body after death. It's just not an option."

"They stuff animals and the like. Why can I not get that done? I'll find the money from somewhere."

"Stop talking like that, May. It's not legal, it's not hygienic and it's not fair on Jacky. Do you think he would want to be stuffed, propped up in your spare room, all day, every day?"

"Maybe he would."

Tam couldn't believe what he was hearing. May had lost the plot. Tam didn't want to hear anymore. He tried to lighten the mood. "He probably would love to be propped up in bed every day. He was a right lazy bastard."

It worked. May was looking at Tam, smiling through the tears. "You're a bit of a lazy bastard yourself, Tam. If work was in bed, you'd sleep on the floor."

May and Tam had a little giggle at this, but May got serious again. "Tam, I know you owe me nothing, but I need you to do me one big favour…"

The favour May asked Tam disturbed him a bit, but Tam promised he'd do it. He just couldn't say no to May. However, he had to put this to one side for the time being. He had to get to Butt before he drove a couple of six-inch nails into Jacky's head.

As he walked to Butt's place of business, Tam thought more and more of where he had seen him before. The thirty-minute walk to the undertakers did the trick. By the time he got there, Tam had realised exactly where he knew the undertaker from.

Tam felt a little uneasy as he walked into the undertakers. He was a little surprised that there was nobody there to greet him. There was no reception area, just a hallway. There were several doors in the hallway, each leading to other rooms. There was something old fashioned about the place, something uncomfortable. It was easy to see that Butt had put no money into modernising his workplace. By the looks of the place, he didn't employ cleaners either. Fifty-year-old wallpaper, fifty-year-old carpet, doors that creaked, dimly lit. An unpleasant place to be at the best of times. Who is ever at an undertakers in good times anyway?

Tam said nothing. Instead, he just started opening doors, looking for Butt. In a couple of the rooms, there were dead bodies in coffins. People who had lived and loved. Tam felt sadness at seeing these people lie in this place, their last place of rest, until they went down a hole forever. He thought how awful it was to live their whole lives just to spend their last days in this shithole. Did their families not want them? Why couldn't they spend these last days of daylight in a family member's home?

He ascertained that the families of these people were bastards. Selfish bastards, no more, no less. As he was thinking these thoughts, he was opening doors, looking for Butt. The third door Tam opened was the door he was looking for – there in front of him, preparing Jacky's body, was Butt. Butt, by chance, had Jacky's toupee in his hand when Tam walked in.

Butt, with his back to the door, never heard Tam come into the room. Tam wasn't long letting him know about his presence though.

"Well, *night rider,*" said Tam, announcing to Butt that he was in the room.

Butt was startled. "Sorry? You're not allowed in here."

"Or is it Bart? Bart the bastard? You have a few aliases."

"You shouldn't be in here! Please leave immediately."

"Is that Jacky?" asked Tam, looking at the table Butt was standing next to, on top of which, Jacky's corpse was lying.

Not waiting for Butt's answer, Tam walked over to the table and saw Jacky laid out on it. Tam was a little shocked, not because of the naked dead friend he was looking at, but because his naked dead friend had no hair on his head.

"Fuck me, he looks like an ugly version of Right Said Fred."

"You'll have to leave, you are not allowed in here." Butt persisted.

Tam was menacing at the best of times, but with Butt, he was particularly menacing. It was as if he hoped Butt would do or say something worth beating him to a pulp for.

"Who's going to make me leave? You?" responded Tam in a threatening manner.

"I'll call the police."

"Go ahead, call them. I'm sure they would love to hear a story or two about you."

"What stories?"

"Don't you remember me, Bart?"

"No, why, should I?"

"You used to work at the city morgue, didn't you?"

Butt ignored the question. He walked over to the sink and started to wash his hands.

Tam continued. "You were the night rider."

"I don't know what you're talking about."

"Why were you called the *night rider*?"

"That was never proven."

"Granted, but I don't think you should be allowed to work with dead people, do you?"

"I'll have you know that I take great care in my work."

"You were stealing drugs from the morgue. Prescription drugs. You had some sort of scam going."

"You have to leave now–"

"I'll never forget the night I was there," interrupted Tam. "It was all a bit sickening for my liking, and I've seen a lot."

"What was sickening?"

"Do you remember Barnsy?"

"Who?"

"Barnsy. He was a mate of mine. He used to buy drugs from you when you worked in the morgue. Although fuck knows what kind of illegal highs are sold out of a morgue."

"I've never sold any drugs in my life," Butt protested.

"Barnsy asked you for a cup of tea. You opened the fridge to get the milk and the milk was sitting in-between the severed feet of a big woman… I know it was a woman because her toenails were painted."

"What's wrong with that? We only had one fridge."

"I said: God love that girl, probably done good all her life, just to end up in a fridge."

"I can't remember any of this."

"I can. I can also remember what you said. *You* said: fuck that fat bastard, she probably spent her whole life in the fridge anyway."

"I did not! I have ethics."

"Ethics? I know why you were called the *night rider*. It doesn't take too much imagination to figure out how someone gets a name like that. Someone like you should be nowhere near the dead."

Tam turned his attention to the Jacky's toupee, which Butt was holding in his hands.

"You're not nailing that to his head."

"How else am I meant to keep it on?"

"I don't know… you're the undertaker… what about Velcro?"

"It won't stick to the skin."

"Listen, Bart the bastard… night rider… or whatever name you're going by these days, I don't care if you've to stand and hold it onto his head for the duration of the wake. You're not fucking nailing it."

"OK, I'll think of something. You're going to have to leave now."

"By the way, she's going to take that expensive coffin, the Diamond Blue one."

Butt couldn't believe his luck. Could this Neanderthal be a sucker? His heightened joy was to be short lived. "Excellent choice, sir. It retails at two thousand. Will she be paying cash, or would she like to take out our repayment plan?"

"She'll be giving you five hundred pounds for it. Cash."

"Oh, no, it's two thousand pounds."

"She'll be giving you four hundred and fifty. Cash."

"No, no, no, that casket is two thousand pounds."

"Didn't I mention? Every time you utter the number 'two thousand', the price you're going to get for it goes down by fifty pounds. So you're actually down to four hundred now."

"Why would I give you a coffin priced at two…" Butt stopped short of saying the number. He continued. "…a coffin, *that price*, for four hundred pounds?"

"It's simple… because I won't then broadcast to everyone who you are, Bart the bastard, the night rider."

By the time Tam had left the undertakers, he had secured the two thousand pound coffin for Jacky. Bart was hesitant but he knew that if word got out about his time in the morgue, it would ruin him. Anyway, four hundred pounds for the coffin was still double the cost price, so he still made a few quid.

Tam left happy. He had got one over on this repulsive person. On his way out, he noticed half a dozen small bags, all with ashes in them. Along with the ashes, each bag contained a picture of an old woman. Sick bastard Bart, Tam thought to himself. He thought about Butt and his thick Irish brogue. He realised that Butt had probably moved here from the south when the troubles were at an all-time high. Making a profit off the dead and grieving. Warped fucker, he thought, but it takes all sorts to make the world.

CHAPTER NINE
TOO MUCH LOVE WILL KILL YOU

Stacey and Jacky were an item right up until his death. They had stopped living together a few years ago, because of Jacky's drink problem. His alcohol abuse never stopped her loving him. She would call, bring him dinner, tidy up, or let him know if she was a little horny. Although the sex wasn't great; Jacky was always under the weather, but she simply didn't want to have sex with anyone else. On the night Jacky died, Stacey needed a little loving. She made him dinner and headed round to his house, not knowing it was the last night they would ever spend together.

It was just like any other night. She would take him dinner. Sometimes they would end up sleeping together, sometimes not. Jacky's door was always open during the day. He had no reason to lock it. He had no enemies, and nothing worth stealing. Stacey made her way up the hall, and popped her head around the door.

"All right, love?"

Jacky was sitting in the armchair. He had a half bottle of cider sitting beside him. A glass, half-filled with the cider, was sitting next to the bottle. He was watching TV when Stacey popped her head in. He was always glad to see her.

"I brought you some dinner." Stacey entered the room holding Jacky's dinner.

"You shouldn't have bothered, Stacey. I'm not eating much these days," protested Jacky, but he was still curious. "What is it, anyway?"

"Pie and salad," Stacey answered, lifting the tin foil that covered the plate, so Jacky could see this culinary delight.

Jacky was a bit perturbed at this curious combination. "Pie and salad? Oh right, thanks."

Stacey could sense Jacky's disapproval of the fare on offer. "Oh, right? What's that supposed to mean?"

Jacky didn't want or need an argument, but he had to put his point across. "I'm not sure pie and salad go together as a meal. That's all I'm saying. No big deal."

"How do they not go together? It's like pie, salad and chips, only there's no chips."

"That's the whole point," Jacky explained. "There are no chips. They just don't go together without chips."

Stacey thought back to the morning with Billy and how he moaned about eggs and mushrooms not going together. What is it with men and food combinations? They'd eat the scabs of a dead dog if they were hungry enough.

"I'll take it back if you don't want it."

"Don't be silly, I'll eat it later."

"No, I'll take it back over to the house. You don't want it."

"I said I'll eat it later. Are you here for an argument?"

Stacey wasn't there for an argument. She was there for sex with her man, so she quickly changed the subject so as not to jeopardise her plans.

"What's that you're watching?"

"Maury Povich."

"I hate him… gives me the creeps," replied Stacey.

"There was a fat girl on it. She's frightened of parrots… some kind of phobia. All this girl must do is never go to Australia, South America or a zoo, and she'll never see a fucking parrot. But, no, she must go into a studio full of them, try to conquer her fear or something. There were about a hundred of the fucking things. She near shit herself. Silly fucker. Should have seen how fat she was, too. I think she also had a phobia of salads, the gym and anything healthy."

"God love her. Must be her glands or something," Stacey said.

"*God love her*? Her mother couldn't love this thing."

Jacky – probably at the smell of the home-cooked pie – suddenly felt a little hungry. He took a sip of cider from his glass, got up and walked to the kitchen, where Stacey had set the pie and salad. He buttered two rounds of bread, lifted the plate of food, scraped the salad into the bin and put the pie in-between the two rounds of bread he had just buttered. He returned to the living room, sat down and ate his pie sandwich.

"Where's the salad?" asked Stacey, noticing the lack of green in the sandwich. "You're not going to eat the salad, then?"

"It looked a bit lettuce-y" Jacky said.

"Lettuce-y? What does that mean?"

"There was just a lot of lettuce on it, that's all."

"What did you do with it?"

"I binned it."

"It could have done you later."

"Later? What for?" asked Jacky. "What would I do with it later?"

"You could have had a salad sandwich."

"Who eats salad sandwiches?"

"I don't know. I'm sure someone does."

"I don't know anyone who does," argued Jacky. "But I know someone who definitely doesn't… me."

"I just don't like wasting food, that's all."

"Stacey, did you come around here to annoy me?"

"No, you know I didn't. I just wanted to bring you dinner."

Jacky was getting a fed up. He hated arguments with Stacey and he felt one brewing. He would never ask her to leave his home. If they were ever arguing, he would leave. He felt he had to leave now to avoid a fight. "I think I'll head on up to bed." Jacky pretended to yawn, so as not to let Stacey think he was leaving the room because of her.

Stacey was quick off the mark. "Do you mind if I join you?" Stacey threw Jacky a wink.

Jacky knew right away what she meant. "For a ride? You know I'm not as able as I used to be, Stacey."

"You'll be OK."

"How will I be OK? I can barely get it up to semi-hard."

"I thought about that… not getting it up the last couple of times we tried… and I got you something. Look."

Stacey opened her hand. There was a Viagra tablet sitting on the palm.

Jacky wasn't keen on the sight of this. "Fuck's sake, I'm on enough medication. I can't take that."

"It's only the one, it'll do you no harm."

"I don't know. It's not just getting it up. I've no energy either."

"You'll be OK once it kicks in. You'll have plenty of energy."

"They don't give you energy… they give you an erection."

"Go on, try it, just this once."

Always a sucker for Stacey, and the thoughts of having a sustained erection, Jacky agreed to take the tablet. After taking it, finishing his sandwich and downing the last of the cider that was in the half-filled glass, Stacey and Jacky headed up the stairs for a little fun, blue diamond style.

After undressing and lying in bed fumbling for about thirty minutes, there was still no rise from Jacky. Both of them were getting frustrated.

"Maybe if you took your socks off?" Jacky said.

"Do you think so?" Stacey took her socks off.

Fifteen minutes later, still nothing happened.

"This isn't working, Stacey. Let's go back downstairs."

"Just give it another wee while, Jacky."

"Nothing's happening… if I'm honest, it's getting a bit embarrassing."

"If I talk dirty, do you think that would help?"

"I don't know, what are you going to say?"

"It won't work if I tell you. It has to be spontaneous. Let's kiss and cuddle another wee while, then I'll start."

While kissing Jacky, Stacey thought for a few minutes about what to say. She had no idea. Then she thought of something, and blurted it out.

"Black man's ballbag."

Jacky stopped what he was doing. "What the fuck was that? Is that your idea of talking dirty? Black man's ballbag? What a passion killer."

"It was the first thing that came into my head."

"That was the first thing that came into your head? A certain black man's ballbag? Or any black man's ballbag? What kind of shit is that? I'm going downstairs to finish my drink."

"Don't go yet! We can try something else."

"Like what? Look at ballbag pictures?"

"I heard a man's erogenous zone is up his backside... what if I insert something up there to get you going?"

"No way!"

"Go on, it'll be nice."

"It'll be nice? Do you think I'm some sort of bender?"

"It doesn't make you gay. All men are into it now."

"What do you intend to stick up me, if you don't mind me asking?"

Stacey dipped her hand into her bag and pulled out a small plastic lighter.

"You're not putting that up me," Jacky said.

"Sure, it's small."

"It might be small but what happens if it blows up inside me? I'll have a black man's ballbag then. Charred black."

"How will it blow up? It's not one of those cheap ones, I paid three pounds for it."

"I don't care how much you paid for it, I'm not chancing it."

Stacey put her hand back into her bag and took out a much larger deodorant can.

Jacky was taken aback. "No way! Look at the size of that thing... it's not going anywhere near my arse."

"I'll just ease it in slowly."

"What do you think I have down there? A sump hole? I'm not letting you near me with that."

Stacey put her hand back into her bag for a third time and took out a pen. "This'll do. It can't explode, and it's thin... it'll go in easy."

"Maybe you could write a romantic love poem on my back passage while it's in there? It's not happening, Stacey. I'm not letting you shove anything up me. This is over... it's not happening tonight. I'm going back downstairs."

Stacey wasn't taking no for an answer tonight. She had one more thing up her sleeve. She dipped her hand back into her bag and took out another Viagra tablet.

"One more thing. If it doesn't work, we'll give it a miss tonight."

"What else is there? Nothing's going to work."

Jacky looked down at Stacey's open palm containing the second tablet.

"Another one? It didn't work the last time… it's hardly going to work this time."

"Double the dose will definitely work."

Jacky was fed up. After a little huffing and puffing, he relented and took the second tablet. After five more minutes of kissing and cuddling, it worked. Jacky was up and at it.

Jacky was on top of Stacey. They were in the missionary position. Stacey was underneath and had her eyes closed. She always had her eyes closed in that position. No reason, just habit. A few minutes in, with Jacky on top, he started spitting at her. This was new, and Stacey liked it. "Go on, spit on me. I'm a dirty bitch."

She got what she wanted. Before long, her forehead and face were soaking wet. It got a bit extreme, so she opened her eyes, and found Jacky a couple of inches from her face. But his eyes were closed, and he was foaming excessively from the mouth. His whole weight suddenly slumped on top of her. He was limp. Stacey knew there was something wrong and she started to panic.

"What the *fuck*?" she said out loud, pushing the motionless Jacky off her.

Jacky slumped onto the bed and Stacey jumped off the bed. She stared at him for a few seconds, not knowing what was going on. Jacky was motionless. She didn't know where to look for a pulse, so she bent down and put her ear to his mouth. There were no signs of breath.

She was now frantic. "Jacky! Jacky. Jacky, wake up. Wake up."

She started pushing at his chest; something she had seen on TV. She slapped his face, trying to waken him. She tried mouth-to-mouth resuscitation. She had really no idea what she to do in a situation like this, so she just copied what she had seen on TV. After a few minutes of trying various things, she gave up. Her panic subsided and she was now numb with sorrow. She lay down beside him, caressing him, stroking him, kissing him. The only thing in the world she loved was now dead.

She lay for what seemed to be hours. In fact, it was about fifteen minutes. Then it dawned on her: it was the tablets. The two Viagra tablets she had given him. The two tablets, mixed with his other medication, had had an adverse reaction to his already weak system.

She had, in fact, killed him. Sorrow quickly turned to self-preservation.

"Jesus Christ, I need to get out of here," she said to herself, jumping off the bed and gathering up her belongings. She thought about phoning an ambulance. But if she phoned an ambulance, she would have to tell them about the double dose of Viagra. She could go to gaol – worse still – the shame. They would talk. Everybody would be talking about it, like they did the last time she shamed herself. That day was the worst day of her life. She would never have got through it without Jacky. But Jacky's gone now. There's no way she could cope. She decided to leave him and phone nobody. It was for the best. Jacky wouldn't want her to go through all that again. If he was here, he would say, 'just leave me'. And that's exactly what she did. She left. She left the love of her life dead on the bed.

****

Stacey rushed home after leaving Jacky's house, crying the whole time. She saw nothing and heard nothing, the whole journey home. When she got through her own front door, she closed the blinds. She knew – although always in denial – that Jacky couldn't have had long to live. Her initial thoughts were selfish: she could go to prison, people would talk, and there would be gossip. And what would May do? May would hate her forever. These thoughts soon subsided. She was, by the time she got home, heartbroken. The reality had kicked in. Jacky's gone. Gone forever.

She poured herself a drink. Pimm's and brown lemonade. She thought, as she poured the drink, about her mother and grandmother, who both enjoyed the same tipple. How she wished one of them was around now to confide in, to seek advice, or for a simple hug. She wanted to be told that everything was going to be all right. She then thought, who is she kidding? She couldn't tell anyone. She had forced a man to take pills for her sexual gratification and he died because of it. She could tell no one; the shame would be the end of her. What will I do? Will I go back? Phone someone? Lots of thoughts were going through her head. She tried to think of anything similar that had happened, to anyone else, but she couldn't. Who accidently dies taking Viagra? It was an accident, she kept telling herself. But there's nothing accidental about shoving Viagra down a sick man's throat.

She decided to say nothing, phone nobody and not to go back to Jacky's house. The word *dead* resonated through her skull and sent shivers down her spine. Fuck, she thought as she sat crying. She had work the next day. In the tea hut. Jacky's mates would be there. They would have heard about Jacky. Would they suspect her? Why would they? No one knew she was there.

Jacky's dead.

She cried until the early hours.

CHAPTER TEN
FRANKY ESCOBAR

Belfast is the capital city of Northern Ireland, or as half the population like to call it, 'The North'. Calling it the 'The North', as most nationalists tend to do, means that they don't recognise, in their minds, the state of Northern Ireland. Of course, it is a state, created by the British in 1921. It's a state with its own laws, created by its own institutions, which everyone living there must abide to.

Belfast has had its fair share of drug-using and drug-dealing through the years, but nowhere near as bad as the drug epidemics of a lot of Europe's capital cities. This was because of the summary execution of suspected drug dealers by the IRA throughout the nineties. It didn't stop people selling drugs, but it made people think twice before they did. Whether this was right or wrong is a matter of opinion. There are so many complexities to the IRA policy. One would have to take every slain individual and examine whether they deserved what was bestowed on them.

A few weeks before Jacky's death, Franky was in work. To be honest, Franky was always in work. He was too mean to miss any days. From an innocent onlooker, this may seem like good work ethic. But he actually spent his days skiving about, going on 'wee walks' under the pretence of looking for something or someone. He would be looking for an engineer, the foreman, trying to borrow tools, anything for a wee dander about.

On one of his paid strolls, he happened upon an overwhelming smell of weed being smoked. Being a nosey bastard, he investigated. Franky didn't care about drugs; he didn't take them. He didn't care who did or who didn't. The scent of the weed being smoked led him to a small room at the back of one of the buildings they were working on. A couple of junior painters and decorators had found themselves a small enclave out of harm's way to enjoy a skive and a little recreational smoke of weed. Franky, needing to show his authority, decided to pull the boys up on their misdemeanour, not that he cared. But he did like throwing his weight about when he could get away with it, much like a bully.

"Well, well, well, what's going on here?" Franky asked, with the smugness and grandeur of an old-fashioned head teacher.

The two boys, having the mislaid notion that there was someone important talking to them, try to hide the joint. "Nothing going on here, Franky. There's an awful smell of blow coming from somewhere. Can you smell it?" replied one of the young men, hiding the joint behind his back.

"Don't take me for an idiot, lads. I can see the spliff burning behind your back." Franky motioned his head toward the joint one of the boys was trying to conceal.

It didn't take too long before they knew that denial would be futile. They were rumbled. In their own minds, however, they overestimated Franky's importance. They tried to explain themselves.

"You'll not say anything, will you, Franky?" one of the young lads asked.

"I'll not say anything. You better watch that shit though. It'll melt your brain."

"It's OK, Franky, it hasn't done us any harm."

Franky looked at the two boys, both gaunt, open-mouthed and zombie-like.

"Right, it does you no harm… the pair of you are living testament to that." Franky quipped sarcastically.

"It's good shit, Franky, do you want a wee smoke?"

"No, I'm OK. This is a warning. I don't want to see you smoking this stuff in work again. If I do, you'll both be sacked."

It was starting to dawn on the two blow heads how unimportant Franky was. "We don't work for you."

"What?"

"You can't sack us… we don't work for you."

"Are you trying to be funny?"

"No, just saying… how can you sack us if we don't work for you?"

"Did I say *I* would sack you?"

"No, but you implied it."

Franky was insulted that this young lad would question his authority. The young lad was right though; Franky had no clout. He couldn't even tell their boss what he had caught them doing. If he did that, he would be the talk of the site – a tout. They were standing up to him now. He couldn't bully them.

Franky begrudgingly decided not to pursue this argument. "I'm away back to work, I'll leave you to it. A bit less of the cheek in the future, or I'll be having a word with your boss."

As Franky started to walk out of the room, he spotted a big bag of weed sticking out of one of the boy's lunch bags. He walked to the bag and lifted out the weed. "What's this then?" Franky knew nothing about drugs, but he wasn't stupid – he knew this amount of grass would be at least a hundred – maybe two hundred – pounds to buy.

"Who owns this?" Franky asked, dangling the drugs in front of the two boys.

The boys refused to answer. They knew rightly that it's one thing having a joint in work, but it's another thing to have that amount of weed in your lunch bag. It could be construed as drug dealing.

"I'll have to confiscate this," said Franky.

"Don't be doing that, Franky. That cost a week's wages," pleaded one of the young men.

"I don't mind you lads having a wee puff in work, but when you bring it in to sell, I have to draw the line."

"We're not selling it. It's to do us all week."

"There's an awful lot here for personal use."

"It's between us, half of it's his." The young man gestured with his head that the other half belonged to his friend.

"I'll do you a favour. I'll take it up to the office. I'll say I found it. You won't get into trouble."

"Fuck's sake Franky, don't be doing that. Give us it back."

"That's the deal. Either that, or I tell them the truth as to how I came across it."

The two young men had twigged Franky was a nothing, but even he could get them into serious trouble if he reported them. They could do nothing but watch Franky walk out of the room with their stash. Franky smiled as he walked out. He had no intentions of handing it over. The only thought in his head was who he could sell it to. It would be a couple of weeks later though that someone would come to mind.

The weed sat in Franky's house for a while. He really had no idea who to sell it to without looking like a dealer. One night it dawned on him that Jacky might buy it. Why not? He was an alcoholic. He might buy it to help him sleep, to ease any pain he's having, or just to get stoned. Yes, he thought, Jacky would buy it. He would go over there, get a hundred quid for it. He would be a hundred pound richer for no work whatsoever. Easy money. He put on his coat and strolled the short way to Jacky's.

As he approached Jacky's house, he could see the Jacky's wheelie bin sitting outside his door. Silly fucker, he thought. Jacky had left his bin out, forgetting about the bank holiday the next day. This also brought to Franky's mind that he himself needed a new wheelie bin – someone had stolen his a few weeks earlier. Maybe the two lads he accosted the drugs from as a form of revenge. He was furious about this, but had no clues as to who the thief was, only suspicions. Jacky would only have a couple of months left in him at most, he thought to himself. He would hold off buying a new wheelie bin, because when Jacky bites the dust, he can come around and take his. This cheered Franky. The thought of not having to buy a new bin put him in good form as he reached Jacky's door.

As he approached Jacky's front door, he noticed it was open. He shouted up the hall, beckoning Jacky. "Jacky? Are you in?"

Franky waited a minute or two, there was no show from Jacky, so he decided to shout again. "Jacky, it's Franky. Are you home?"

This time, Franky's shouting had the desired effect. Jacky came to the door. He was gaunt and half asleep. He was also curious as to why Franky was at his home.

"Franky? What's the craic? Come on in."

Jacky walked up the hall, Franky following behind mumbling small talk. They both sat down in the living room.

Franky started feigning concern about Jacky's health. "How are you doing, buddy? You keeping all right? Still not back to work yet?"

"Nah, Franky, I'm not able for work these days. I'm just glad to see the light of day in the mornings, if I'm honest."

"You still on the drink?"

Jacky looked at Franky then at the half bottle of cider and half-filled glass sitting in front of them. What a stupid question, he thought. Jacky didn't even bother answering.

Both men sat in silence for a couple of minutes. Jacky had no idea why Franky was in his house.

Franky broke the silence. "Is that your feet I smell?"

Jacky had had enough. "Why are you here, Franky?"

"No reason. I called to see how you're doing."

"You never call. What do you want?"

"I'm worried about you. Do you not believe me?"

"No."

"Then if I'm not worried about you, why would I bring you around this?"

Franky produces the weed as if he was producing some miracle cure for Jacky's condition. "What is it?" asked Jacky, knowing what it was but wondering why Franky had brought it.

"I was concerned about your drinking, so I brought you some weed to try to ween you off the drink."

Jacky took the weed off Franky and examined it. "Where did you get this?"

"I bought it… had you in mind. I don't use it myself, but as I say, it could get you off that drink."

"I don't know about that, Franky. It could be a case of out of the frying pan into the fire."

"Nonsense! A wee smoke will do you no harm. It's good for arthritis."

"I haven't got arthritis."

"It's good to keep you calm."

"I'm always calm."

"It must be good for something, otherwise it wouldn't be so expensive. Roll one up, Jacky."

"I can't be bothered, Franky, it's not my thing."

"Go on, roll one. There's papers sitting there. Skin one up."

Jacky now had the feeling Franky wasn't going to go home until he skinned up a joint. He also didn't want to seem ungrateful at Franky's generous gesture. Jacky skinned up then lit up a joint.

Franky, mid-conversation, was distracted by the forty-two-inch TV that sat in Jacky's living room. It looked new.

"Did you get a new TV, Jacky?"

"I did. Got it on finance. I'm paying it off."

Franky wondered what would happen to the TV when Jacky died. He surely only had a couple of months. Would his mother, May, get it? Will they take it back if it's not paid? As Jacky smoked, Franky pondered for a little while about how he could get his hands on the TV. Such thoughts would have to be put on hold; there were more pressing issues.

"Is it good stuff, Jacky? What do you reckon?"

"I suppose it's OK."

"I told you it was good stuff. Have you the hundred quid there?"

"What hundred quid?"

"A hundred quid for the grass. It's half price; there must be two hundred pounds' worth there."

"Where the fuck would I get a hundred pounds?"

"You didn't think I was giving it away for free, did you?"

"Yes, as a matter of fact, I did."

"I'm only asking for the money I paid for it. I'm making nothing on it."

"Listen to me, Franky, I haven't got a hundred pounds. If I had, I sure as fuck wouldn't be spending it on this shit."

Jacky throws the bag of grass back over to Franky. Franky takes it, then looks at the joint Jacky's smoking.

"What, Franky? Do you want this back, too?"

"There's at least a fiver's worth there."

"And what? Are you looking me to give you a fiver for this joint? The joint you coaxed me to take?"

"No, of course not. Smoke away, it's on the house."

"Jesus, Franky, for a minute there, I thought that you actually gave a fuck about how I was keeping."

"I do give a fuck! I went out and bought it for you, didn't I?"

"Did you, fuck! You probably found it, or got it dirt cheap."

Franky was a little embarrassed. Now he'd been caught at his work, he decided to change the subject. "Big Tam and your ma still thick?"

"Don't be starting any of your shite, Franky. There's nothing going on with Tam and my ma. She sees him like a son."

"I didn't mean it like that."

"Yes, you did. Trying to be smart. Say another word about it and I'll tell Tam."

"Don't be saying anything to him, Jacky. He's a beast. Do you remember the day me and you were on that job and he knocked that Alsatian out with one punch?"

"I remember it well, Franky. Why did he knock the dog out? Can you remember?"

"Remember the guy with the big beard? Jim, or Jimmy… or something. He had a Polish guy working for him. Jim used to bring the Pole and his own dog to work every morning. Don't know why he brought the dog. He used to have all his tools on the back seat. He lived about an hour and a half drive away from the job. One morning, when they pulled up to the job, Tam saw the Pole get out of the boot while the dog sat in the front seat!"

"You're kidding me? The Polish guy was in the boot for an hour and a half? The dog sat, like a fucking lord, in the front?"

"Yep. Tam saw the Pole getting out of the boot. He was disgusted, played on his mind all day. He waited until home time then approached the car. The Polish guy was just about to get into the boot for the journey home. Tam walked over and told him he wasn't to get into the boot, he was to get into the front seat. The guy explained that he couldn't because the dog was in the front seat, sitting like a lord. Tam walked over to the dog, gave it a punch, knocked it out, lifted it off the seat and placed it in the boot."

"What about the guy the Pole worked for? Did he not say anything?"

"Of course he didn't! Have you never seen the size of Tam?"

Both men laugh out loud at the story.

"Big Tam… he's mad as a hatter when he starts."

"The next day, the man pulled up for work. The dog was back in the front and there was no Pole in the boot. The bastard sacked him."

"He sacked him? What happened then?"

"Big Tam knocked him out."

"You should be telling that story to an audience, Franky. You're good at telling them. You should have been a stand-up comedian."

"You're kidding! Do you think so? I always wanted to try a bit of stand-up, never got the chance. I was thinking of going to one of those open-mic nights. Do you really think I could do stand-up, Jacky?"

"No."

"What?"

"No."

"Why did you say it then?"

"I was being sarcastic, Franky. You're the most unlikeable person I know."

"Fuck me, there's no call for that."

"I'm just saying."

"I don't care. First chance I get, I'm going to do it. You have to follow your dreams."

"Go for it then. I just don't think you're stand-up material."

"I'm not auditioning here, Jacky. You're not Simon Cowell. I didn't ask your opinion anyway."

"You did."

"Well, maybe I did, but you could have lied at least."

The two men sat talking about the old characters they knew from the building sites. Jacky was enjoying the chat. It was good to catch up, even if it was with Franky. As they talked, Jacky finished his joint. He was enjoying the evening and thought he'd skin up another.

"Give me that grass, Franky. I'll have another wee joint... you're right, they're not bad."

"Fiver."

"What?"

"The first one was free... the next one's a fiver."

"Wise up, don't be so fucking mean. I haven't got a fiver."

"You can owe me it."

"Jesus, Franky, how lousy can someone be? OK, I'll owe you a fiver."

"When?"

"When what?"

"When will you give me it?"

"Friday. I get my money on Friday, I'll give you it then."

"Where?"

"Where *what*?"

"Where will I see you? So, you can give me it?"

"Are you serious?" Jacky looked at Franky. He could see that Franky was deadly serious. "I'll give it to you when you next call."

"I'm busy next week. I might not get around."

"I was only joking, I know you won't be calling. I'll get my ma to bring it round to yours. I'll tell her I borrowed it, OK?"

Franky gave Jacky enough grass for another joint. As Jacky started to skin up, Franky realised that there was not much point hanging about. He wasn't going to shift the weed. Jacky was skint. He decided it was time to go.

"I'm going to head off, Jacky. Can I pop to the toilet before I go?"

"Go ahead, but I don't think there's any toilet roll."

"Why would I need toilet roll?"

"In case you're having a dump."

"Why would I have a dump?"

"I don't know what you're going to the toilet for Franky. I'm just saying, there's no toilet roll. I think there's kitchen roll in there, if you want to take some to the toilet with you."

"I don't need kitchen roll, Jacky. I'm not taking a dump. Who takes a dump in other people's houses anyway? I'm going for a piss."

Franky made his way to the downstairs toilet, leaving Jacky in the living room, enjoying his new-found pleasure. When Franky came out of the toilet, he went straight for the door.

"Right, Jacky, I'm going to shoot off. Make sure May brings that round to me on Friday."

From where Jacky was standing, he could only see the back of Jacky's head. Jacky was still sitting on the chair that Franky had left him in.

"I said I'm away," Franky repeated, a little louder than before.

Franky was a bit peeved that he was being ignored. He walked over to Jacky's chair to confront his rudeness. Jacky was motionless. He was gaunt, eyes sunken and closed.

Franky shook him. "Jacky? Jacky, wake up."

Franky knew there was something wrong. He didn't look like he was napping. He looked like he was dead. When this thought occurred, Franky's first thought was about getting his fiver back, but he knew that even for him this was a new low to think something like that in this situation.

After trying to rouse him for a while, Franky gave up. He took out his phone to call an ambulance. Just before he rang the emergency services, he glanced at the floor. The joint lay there. It had burnt out. Maybe the joints had something to do with him dying? If he is dead, Franky thought to himself, the post mortem would find drugs in his system, and there would be an investigation. No fucking way could a couple of joints have killed him, but maybe, just maybe, they did. Supplying drugs, possession of drugs… maybe murder or manslaughter. Better be safe than sorry, Franky thought. He decided not to phone anybody. As he left, he glanced at the TV. For a fleeting second, he thought about taking it, but he thought better of it though. Theft on top of supplying drugs and murder would be a right mess. Franky left Jacky's house. He never phoned an ambulance.

Franky was calm as he left Jacky's. The joints may have tipped him over the edge and killed him, but he was on his way out anyway. Although Franky accepted that he had a hand in Jacky's final demise, it was coming anyway, he told himself. If he hadn't abused his body so much, would two joints have killed him? No, they wouldn't have, so it was all his own fault. Franky still had a slight worry though. What if they could connect him to the death? Hardly, he thought.

They're not going to send the flying squad out to investigate the death of someone like Jacky. What if some jumped up doctor found drugs in his system? All his mates would swear that he didn't take drugs; maybe they would investigate. They could never prove anything. What if they suspected him? He would have to pay solicitors' fees, take time off work for court, the financial cost would be endless. Right, he thought, get all that shit out of your head. Jacky's dead and there's no bringing him back. It had nothing to do with him, and that's the end of that. Now, about the grass Jacky didn't buy – who might buy it now? This played on his mind for the rest of the night.

CHAPTER ELEVEN
TAM WANTS A WORD

Tam worried about May. He would often call in on her to see how she was doing. He hated seeing her distressed. She was becoming increasingly distressed at Jacky's drinking problem, his failing demeanour and his health in general. She knew her son, and she also knew, without Jacky telling her, that he wasn't at all well. Tam would call for a catch up, a cup of tea and a chat. May would protest every time he called: "Don't be going out of your way to see me, you've better things to do." But the truth was, she loved him calling. She liked the company. Jacky didn't call often, and she disliked going to Jacky's to watch him sit in the chair, drinking his life away. Tam called to see her on this day. None of the two of them knew, however, that Jacky was going to die that night.

May was putting the kettle on when Tam called. He noticed straight away that there was something wrong. She seemed down, depressed or something. He couldn't put his finger on it, so he asked her.

"Are you all right, May?"

"The usual, son. Jacky. I called in to see him earlier. He looks terrible."

"He's a big lad, May, He'll be OK."

"I know my own son, Tam, I know he couldn't have long left. I'm not stupid."

"That's nonsense, May. He'll out-live us both."

"You're a good boy, Tam. I know you mean well, but there really is no use kidding ourselves."

Tam knew that May wasn't one bit stupid. To tell her Jacky was OK and that there was nothing wrong with him would be an insult to her intelligence.

He sat down beside her on the settee and put his arm around her. "Do you want a cup of tea, May?"

"Don't bother yourself, son, I'll make it." May tried to get up from the chair but Tam got up before her.

"You sit there, May. I'll make it."

A few minutes later, Tam was back in the living room holding two mugs of tea. He sat back down beside her.

"How did it get this far, Tam? It seems like only yesterday I was fighting with the other mothers in the second-hand shop, trying to get him the best of the stuff that came in. We hadn't a penny, you know." May started to perk up a little with the thoughts of the second-hand shops years ago. "What were we like? They used to throw in the boxes with all the second-hand clothes in them. We were like vultures. My gorgeous baby boy sat in his pram. He probably thought we weren't wise, a load of women fighting over someone else's rubbish. They were good days. Even though we had no money, we had each other and our health."

"There's no mother could have done any better than you, May. He'll be fine, he's just having a bad turn. He'll pull himself out of it."

"No, Tam, not this time. I can feel it. A mother can sense things about her children. This time, I sense that he's on borrowed time."

"Do you think that there's a selfishness about people that abuse alcohol, May?"

"What do you mean?"

"Drink, drugs, cigarettes. Because these things do harm and are basically self-inflicted problems, do you think it's selfish of them to expect the same level of treatment in hospital as people with, say, leukaemia?"

"I know what you're saying, son. People get cancer… they fight tooth and nail to save themselves, probably never smoked or drank in their lives, then there's Jacky. All he has to do is stop drinking… he can't even do that."

"Addiction's a terrible thing, May. A person needs strong inner strength to overcome it. Jacky just hasn't got what it takes."

"He used to be strong, Tam. Did you know he went off the drink a couple of years ago? For about six weeks."

"I didn't know that, May."

"He was doing brilliant! He started getting fit. He wasn't good at running, so he used to go to the swimmers. Every night he would go. Without fail. He was like a new man… he got the colour back in his face. He was reborn."

"What happened? Why did he quit?"

"One night, he was swimming. He used to swim, up and down, up and down, minding his own business. He was going up and down one night… he was at the edge lane and a heavy girl was getting out of the pool. She was trying to heave herself up the pool ladders. She couldn't hold on. She slipped and fell back into the water, right on top of Jacky. She near enough pinned him to the floor of the pool. It done his back in. He could barely move for a couple of days. That's all it took; a couple of days of boredom put him back on the drink. He never went back to the swimmers."

"Did she not apologise?"

"I don't know, son. Sure, it was nobody's fault."

"I think it was that girl's fault… if she didn't overeat, she would have been able to exit the pool properly. Funny how life is, May. If that girl hadn't have decided to get out of the pool at that second, Jacky could still be off the drink."

"You can't talk like that, son. If one of us, or Jacky, turned a different corner on another day, we could be knocked down, or have any other sort of accident."

"You're right, May. We never know what's ahead of us."

"Go on home, son. You've better things to be doing than sitting here with me."

"There's nothing better than having a yarn with you, May. I have to go, anyway. I have a few things to do."

Tam said goodbye. He had something to do alright. He had to see Jacky. The state May was in was killing Tam. He adored that woman, and he had to try something. Anything. He decided that the only person in control of this situation was Jacky.

****

Tam was calm when he arrived at Jacky's door. He promised himself, for the sake of May, that he wouldn't get angry. He knocked the door a few times and, as usual, it took Jacky a while to answer. "All right, Tam. You looking for my ma? She's not here."

"No, I just left her. Is it OK if I have a word, Jacky?"

"No problem. Come on in."

The first thing to hit Tam as he walked up the hallway was the stench of blow. The whole house stunk of it.

"Fuck, Jacky, are you smoking blow now? Is your head not melted enough?"

"Franky came round trying to sell it. I took a couple of joints. It wasn't too bad."

"What? Is he dealing drugs now?"

"No, he came off with some spiel about buying it for me. He was worried about me, probably stole it off someone. What can I do for you Tam?"

"It's your ma, Jacky, I'm worried about her."

"Why? What's the matter? Is she alright? Is she ill?"

"No, no, nothing like that. She's worried about you. You're not looking the best, Jacky."

"Me? She's worried about, me? I'm OK. I feel a bit rough after those two joints… knocked me clean out. Franky was here when I passed out, I think. I had to check he hadn't taken anything, you know what he's like."

"I'm not talking about what you look like tonight. I'm talking about what you look like all the time now. Look at you, your face is yellow. I've never seen you so thin, you're a mess."

"I've told her a million times, I'm OK. She's sending you round now?" snapped Jacky, clearly irritated.

"She never sent me round, Jacky. You know I don't care what you do to yourself. I'm worried about her."

"You drink twice as much as me, Tam. I don't think you should be preaching to anybody."

"I'm not preaching. You're right, I love a drink as much as anybody, but it's not about me, is it? The time will come when I must deal with the consequences of my drinking, but at the minute, it's not about you or me. It's about your mother."

"You're right Tam, *my* mother, not yours. Just keep your nose out of my business."

Jacky defiantly took a swig of cider from the glass that had been sitting there around three hours now. Tam was starting to get wound up. Jacky was deliberately baiting him.

Jacky wasn't usually this provocative, but the effects of the Viagra and the joints were having an impact on the way he was thinking.

"There's no call to talk to me like that, Jacky. You know what your ma means to me. She doesn't deserve any of this, it's killing her."

"How *do* you feel about her, Tam? That's what I want to know. You've slept with a lot of old blades in your time – some older than my ma, no doubt. So are you trying to wangle your way into her bed?"

"Don't be so fucking sick. If you weren't ill, I'd flatten you, right here, right now. That's your mother you're talking about… show a bit of respect."

"I'm not saying anything about my mother. It's you… she wouldn't look twice at you, even at her age."

"Listen, you sick fuck. Are you going to go off the drink and give yourself a chance? Get your act together? Or are you going to let that fat bird in the swimming pool ruin your life?"

"She told you about that?"

"She mentioned it earlier."

"She shouldn't have. I don't like my health being discussed by outsiders."

"I'm hardly an outsider."

"Why's that, Tam? I'm her son, not you. Why do you take such an interest in my ma, anyway?"

"She's always had my back. She did right by me when I was a kid… I've never forgotten it."

"What did she do? What did she do when you were a kid, Tam?" Jacky was being a little condescending now.

"It's none of your business, Jacky."

"It's none of my business? But my state of health is *your* business?"

"It is when it concerns your mother."

"No, it isn't. It has nothing to do with you."

"She's my friend. A good friend."

"Tam, unless you tell me exactly what she did for you, I'm going to assume you're after her, chasing her… maybe you want to marry her? You'll be my step-da' then, Tam. Maybe, when you're my dad, after you marry my ma, I'll talk to you about my health. Until then, get the fuck out of my house."

Tam was furious with Jacky. It never ever crossed his mind that anything between May and himself could be construed as sleazy. He was starting to bite. He was nearing the zone. He had to leave. "I'm going to leave now. If I have to sit here any longer, listening to that bollocks, I'll fucking swing for you, you cheeky, disrespectful bastard."

Jacky knew who he was dealing with here. Tam usually took no prisoners, but he couldn't help himself. It had to be the drugs pulling his strings now. He decided to have one more dig at him. "Just go," said Jacky, "and make sure you control yourself when it comes to my ma."

That was it. Tam flipped. He had heard enough. It took just one punch. Jacky crashed against the wall and fell to the floor. Tam looked at him. He didn't care. At that moment, he was in the zone – the zone where nothing mattered. He could see nothing, hear nothing, feel nothing. The anger had triggered it. The anger of Jacky's total lack of respect and understanding of May and Tam's relationship. He was about to kick him in the head, but he refrained. He walked out into the hall, about to leave. Then he walked back into the living room where Jacky lay unconscious. Tam kicked him in the head.

Tam left Jacky in a heap. It was the third time that night that Jacky was left unconscious. By the time Tam got home, he was out of the zone. He now realised the consequences of his action. He wasn't worried about Jacky or himself; he was worried about May. Poor May, he thought. Would she ever forgive him? He phoned an ambulance anonymously. He sent it to Jacky's house but he knew he had killed him. The ambulance was too little too late, although it was the right thing to do. He knew that if, by some remote chance, Jacky was alive, then Tam would surely go to jail. Tam wanted him to live, even if Jacky told them everything, which would mean Tam would go down for it. He didn't want May to hurt one second longer than necessary. GBH, assault, attempted murder – he didn't care. But he wanted Jacky to be alive.

If Jacky was dead and there was no one to tell the tale, and if he didn't go to jail, he would look after May. He would go off the drink, start clean-living. He knew he was kidding himself with these thoughts. He was never going to stop drinking. If he got closer to May because of Jacky's death then he would just do the same as Jacky; drink himself to death and May would have to go through it all over again. It was a terrible night for Tam with all of these thoughts running through his head. He couldn't sleep, so he drank.

CHAPTER TWELVE
MEET THE KING

Believe it or not, The King was actually a king. He was The King of the Dudu Tribe – a tribe of about sixteen families from Burkina Faso, a country in West Africa. He also called himself a doctor. Although he had no qualifications, people reckoned he was some sort of witch doctor. He could do some strange things. The King was a supremely confident person. Some say cocky, but he wasn't. He minded his own business and didn't suffer fools gladly. Although they hadn't seen each other in years because their lives took totally different directions, The King and Jacky considered each other best friends. They met in Devon when they were young lads in their early twenties. Jacky was over working, like a lot of Irish men back in the day. He was digging graves, getting himself a wage. When we think of grave-diggers, we think of a couple of workers digging holes with shovels and spades. In reality, graves are now dug with small diggers. Shovels are used to maybe check the digger isn't going too far into a grave that's occupied, or sometimes used to tidy up after the machine's finished. If it was digging graves by hand, Jacky or The King would not have been interested in such employment.

Jacky met The King in a bar in Devon. Jacky was propped up against the bar, having a pint after work. He noticed a thinly-built black lad sitting in the corner. The King was sitting there, just sitting there. Reading nothing, looking at nothing. At first, Jacky thought it was some sort of meditation. He quickly ruled this out; he knew that this lad was aware of everything around him. He didn't know why, but he just knew he was aware of everything, and he was right.

An old man sat at a table. He had a paddy cap on. He was sipping his pint, minding his own business, when three intoxicated men came in. These men were bigger and older than The King. They ordered a drink. They were loud and boisterous. At first, they started looking over at The King. For some reason, they decided not to pursue any shenanigans with him. Then they looked at Jacky. They thought that, because Jacky was a big man, they wouldn't bother him either. Instead, they turned their unwanted attentions to the old man who sat with his half-pint of stout, minding his own business.

"Old timer, do you want a drink?" asked one of the three men.

"No, son, I'm OK," replied the old man.

"Go on, take a wee drink for the road." The men smirked at each other.

"Really, son, I'm fine. I'll drink this and go home."

"You'll take a drink. I'll not take no for an answer."

The old man just wanted a quiet drink, but the man was persistent, so the old man gave in and accepted the drink. "OK, son, I'll take a half glass of Guinness."

"Good man. Barmaid, give the old man a half of Guinness."

The barmaid obliged.

The old man thanked the man for the gesture and continued sipping his drink.

About twenty minutes later, the mouthpiece out of the three men – the one who got the old man a drink – ordered another round. Three pints and a half of Guinness. When asked for payment, he pointed to the old man.

"He's paying. It's his round."

"Oh, no, son. I've no money."

"You take a drink off us and you haven't the money to buy one back?"

"I'm sorry, son… I didn't know you wanted me to buy one back."

"What do you think I am? A fucking charity? Help the aged?"

The old man was embarrassed and a little frightened at this stage.

The mouthpiece walked over to him. "You've no money? How are you going to pay for the drink I bought you?"

"I'm sorry, son, you can have it back."

The mouthpiece looked at the half-glass of Guinness. There was a drink out of it. "Take it back? What am I going to do with it now, what with your geriatric slabbers all over it?"

Jacky stood at the bar. He turned with his elbow on the counter, watching what was happening. He was contemplating intervening but decided he would leave it another minute. Maybe they were just winding the old boy up. The thing Jacky noticed the most was The King. The King sat staring at the situation. No emotion. Just staring.

"Well, old man? Are you buying this drink or what?" The mouthpiece looked like he wasn't going to take no for an answer.

The old man sat silently, quietly frightened.

The mouthpiece took the cap off the old man's head. "I'll just take this then, as payment. It's worth fuck all, like yourself. It looks like rain outside. It'll stop my gel getting messed up."

The King sat watching. As soon as the lad took the cap off the old man's head, he spoke. "That's not yours. Give it back to the person who owns it," said The King, looking directly into the eyes of the troublemaker, who was now wearing the paddy cap, thinking it was a funny thing to do. This lad was about two feet bigger and seven or eight inches wider than The King. The three men turned and looked at The King. They stopped laughing.

Jacky was watching everything. This idiot's going to get killed, he thought. Jacky was ready; he wasn't going to let this young man take these three on alone. He eyed up the two bigger men, he would go for those two first. The young black guy could take the smallest of the three.

"It's not yours either," said the mouthpiece to The King, rather tamely.

"I'll not tell you again. Give it back to the person who owns it," replied The King.

There was something about The King, the way he looked at you, transfixed. His whole manner was mesmerising. Some say it was his witch-doctoring. He had a hypnotic hold over those he spoke to. The man, who was wearing the cap, took it off and offered it to The King.

"Why are you giving it to me? I don't own it. Do I look like someone who would wear a cap?" The King was not looking at the cap, but staring into the eyes of the person holding it.

The mouthpiece looked over to the old man, who was sitting silently, and offered him his cap back. The old man reached out his hand to accept his property back but, before he could take it, The King spoke again.

"Put it back where you got it."

"What?" said the mouthpiece, puzzled.

"Put the cap back where you got it. On his head."

The lad placed the cap back on the old man's head. He even fixed it and positioned it as it was before he took it off. And that was it. The three lads tamely finished their drinks and, without saying much more, left. The King just sat where he was looking at nothing.

When the yobs left, Jacky approached the young man. "You took a chance there."

The King didn't answer.

"Three big fuckers there. You could have been killed."

Again, no answer.

"Do you want a drink?"

"No, thank you," answered The King.

"OK, no problem."

As Jacky walked back to his pint, The King asked him a question. "Is there any work about?"

Jacky stopped, he walked back. "What do you do?"

"Anything."

"What's your name?"

"The King."

"Seriously, what's your name?"

"The King."

"Jim King, Peter King, Pat king? What's your first name?"

"The."

"OK then, King…"

"The."

"What?"

"It's *The* King."

"Sorry, *The* King. There may be a start… guy working with me is going home for good tomorrow. Might not be for you though."

"I'll take it."

"You don't even know what it is."

"I don't care, I'll take it."

"It's digging graves. Would you have a problem with that? What with you being The King and all."

"Why would I? The stiff's gotta to go somewhere."

"No problem. Start with me in the morning."

They arranged to meet him the next day. Jacky drove the digger and The King used the shovel. They became the best of friends.

****

After a few months in Devon, the work dried up. It seemed that nobody was dying and those who were dying were opting for cremation.

On their last day of work, they decided to go for a pint.

"We'll head up to Elgin for work," suggested The King.

"Elgin? Where the fuck's Elgin?" replied Jacky, not having a clue where The King was talking about.

"It's in Scotland."

"Scotland? Why would we go to Scotland?"

The King had done his homework. "It's one of the most densely populated places in Britain for senior citizens."

"And what?"

"There has been a horrendous cold snap up there. The houses are Victorian."

"Again, and what?"

"Old people die when they get cold. Twenty per cent more than at other times. There will be surplus graves to be dug. We can charge a fortune… they can't leave these old dead people lying about. They need someone to put them down their respective holes."

Jacky was shocked. The King, when they weren't working and the library was opened, spent a lot of time there. The same time Jacky spent at the bar. He was reading up on shit and just might have something here.

It didn't take him long to make up his mind. "Good thinking, The King, Elgin it is then. We'll get the bus today."

And there it was. They travelled the length and breadth of Britain for a couple of years, scanning weather reports, census data, newspaper reports of suspected serial killers – anything that brought the death toll up, they would be there, shovels in hand.

They made very good money. The King would go for the odd drink at the weekends, but mostly saved his money. He wasn't going to be digging graves for the rest of his life. Jacky didn't save. He was in the bar every night. The King bought himself a vehicle, a trailer and a small digger. They could dig three or four times more graves with the extra digger machine. The graveyards usually only supplied one machine and, when busy, sub-contracted another firm to dig the extra ones. Now they could dig them all. The King still split everything down the middle.

Jacky got complacent though. He took The King for granted. He would come into work after a night of drinking and The King would have two graves dug with his machine. Jacky would stand and watch him dig another. He'd be half drunk but he would get half the money for doing next to nothing.

****

One day, as The King was digging graves with his machine, Jacky stood watching, hungover.

The King had news. "We have five bookings, Jacky. You have to dig them. I'm going to Africa for a while."

"Why are you going back to Africa?"

"It's my tribe. There's five weddings. I must bless them. They have them all at the same time so I don't have to travel back and forth. I am a real king there you know."

"I know you are. Suppose it can't be helped. If you've to go, you've got to go."

"Will you stay off the drink, Jacky? Just until I come back. I don't want you messing around in the digger drunk. I'll be back in a week."

"Don't you worry about that. Go you over… enjoy your family. I'll see you when you come back. I'll sort it."

Of course, it wasn't sorted. The King went back to Africa to tend to his business, and Jacky lost all five bookings. The morning The King left, Jacky got into the digger half drunk. He swung the bucket and accidently smashed two of the neighbouring graves' headstones. He was told he wasn't to drive the digger again. He had to dig them by hand. It took him three days to dig one. He had a small amount of dirt to take out of it one morning when he fell asleep drunk. If it wasn't for an eagle-eyed mourner, the coffin would have been placed on top of him at the burial. The bookings were lost.

When The King returned a month later, Jacky was gone. He'd headed home. They never saw each other for years after. It was a blessing for The King. Without having to give the freeloading Jacky half of his earnings, he could expand his grave-digging empire. Soon he was employing people to dig graves all over the country. The King was always one to better himself. He took night classes in computing at the same time as expanding his business. At least five or six people would ask him every day for directions while he dug graves. Do you know where plot A is? What about plot B? Do you know where my mother is buried? It didn't take The King long to twig there was money to be made. He developed a find-a-grave app where, for the meagre sum of five pounds, you could download an app with all of the relevant data to show you a map of the graveyard and bring you directly to your loved one's grave – any grave, anywhere in the country. This app made him a lot of money. Jacky knew all about this through second- and third-hand parties. He was never jealous. Instead, he was proud of his prodigy. He had pride but he was embarrassed that they had both had the exact same chance in life, and The King chose a path, and Jacky chose a path. The King succeeded, and Jacky was a drunk. The King tried, on numerous occasions, to contact Jacky. Jacky always dodged him because he was embarrassed.

Jacky, about a fortnight before he died, decided to contact The King. Jacky wasn't at all stupid; he knew he hadn't much time left on this Earth. He wanted to tell The King how proud he was of him, and that he regarded him as his only friend. The King was delighted and agreed to meet him. He booked into a hotel not far from where Jacky lived, and he visited him every night. They would chat and laugh about the old days. Jacky asked The King to do one thing for him. He wanted to see him in private. Jacky requested that The King visited in the evening and, if anyone was in the house when he called, he'd have to come back later. The King wasn't allowed to let May know who he was. Jacky didn't want May to know how successful his old mate was, and that they started out together. It would only reiterate to his mother how much of a loser he really was.

On the night Jacky died, The King came to his door, as he did the previous eight nights. He would always look through the gaps in the blinds. He did this for a couple of reasons. Firstly, if Jacky was asleep, he would let him rest and call back later. Secondly, The King was making sure nobody was with Jacky, respecting Jacky's wishes not to introduce himself.

The King pulled up a little way down the street in his BMW. He walked the short distance to Jacky's door and had a peek through the blinds. Jacky was sat in the chair. He could also see a woman holding a plate. At first glance, he thought pie and salad was on the plate with no chips. He convinced himself it must be something else; no one eats pie and salad without chips. Was this Stacey? Jacky had spoken of her. Tasty wee thing, he thought. Jacky was punching above his weight. Fair play to him. The King decided to leave. Jacky had a visitor so he'd call back later.

An hour or so later, he decided to call again. This time, as he drove down the street, he spotted someone at Jacky's door. The King didn't know Franky. Jacky's popular tonight, he thought. He decided to drive on by, leave it another hour or two then call back. Upon his return, as he rolled down the street in his BMW, he could see a man emerging from Jacky's house. He hadn't a clue who this person was. It was, of course, the third visitor that night: Tam. The King decide to give it a couple of minutes, in case this visitor forgot something and decided to come back. With all the comings and goings at Jacky's house, The King would have presumed he had died. He wasn't dead though; The King had seen him earlier that night. He was sitting there while Stacey stood with the pie and salad. The King made a phone call while waiting to make sure Tam didn't return. He phoned a waiter he knew to see if anyone ever ordered pie and salad with no chips. The phone call lasted about seven minutes and, as The King hung up, he was stunned to see an ambulance roll up at Jacky's door. Unbeknown to The King, it was the ambulance Tam phoned when he got home.

By the time the ambulance came, Jacky was still on the floor. He had just about regained consciousness. The ambulance crew and The King entered Jacky's house together. The King informed the crew of Jacky's illnesses, all sorts of drink-related problems including advanced stages of cirrhosis of the liver. Jacky was brought out of the house in a wheelchair. He was talking, or slurring, to be more precise. The King followed the ambulance up to the hospital in his car. They had Jacky in the emergency theatre for about an hour before he died. The King never got a chance to speak to him, never got a chance to hear the story of how the night unfolded.

The King gave the name and address of May to the doctors after being told that Jacky had died. The King left the hospital before May and Ted arrived. There was no autopsy or post mortem. The death was put down to liver failure caused by advanced stages of cirrhosis.

On his way back to the hotel, The King was perturbed. He knew one of the people who visited Jacky that night had done something to bring forward Jacky's demise. There were at least two there after Stacey, but did they do? Was it Stacey? Did Stacey do something to bring it on? Then there was the skitter at the door on his second visit – he looked a bit sinister. Fly-looking wee fucker, he thought. And there was the big lad on his third visit. Did he call for something? The ambulance came not long after he was there. Had he called it? That big fella? The King would hang about for the funeral. He would have to get to the bottom of his. Even though the death certificate would read natural causes, there was something that wasn't right.

CHAPTER THIRTEEN
THE FUNERAL

The old Irish ritual of burial consists of the funeral cortege, along with the body, walking from the home of the deceased to the chapel. If the deceased is popular, you could get thousands at the funeral. If he is unpopular, there would be far fewer people. It is a very awkward time for the families of those getting buried. It's the mark of a man, how many attend a funeral. The deceased doesn't care of course; they're dead. The embarrassment lies with the living, if there isn't a good attendance.

Jacky's turnout wasn't bad. A lot of people he worked with through the years attended. This didn't mean they all cared about him. Some did, but others took advantage of getting a couple of hours away from work. Bosses wouldn't usually dock pay for a funeral if their workers were back within a couple of hours.

Donned in their black attire, Martin, Ted, Franky and Tam walked together behind the coffin. Another funeral ritual is that, on the way to the chapel, all of the men present take a lift. Four men would be picked from the cortege, and each takes a corner of the coffin. They walk about fifty metres, then swap for another four, then another four, and so on, until the hearse reaches the chapel. The undertaker would organise these lifts. He would walk behind the hearse and, every so often, he would pick four men out of the mourners to relieve the previous four. The fewer mourners at a funeral, the longer your lift was.

The undertaker, Bart the bastard, was organising the lifts on the way to the chapel. Ted, Franky, Martin, and Tam were called to the front; it was their turn for a lift. They took their positions, one at each corner, and started the sombre walk. Franky, of course, wasn't happy at the way he and the other three were positioned when they started to carry the coffin. Bart had placed the two smallest men, Franky and Martin, at the back of the coffin. Ted and Tam were at the front, meaning that the stronger ones were not spread equally. Franky wasn't pleased.

"Ted, my shoulders killing me. It's taking all the weight back here," moaned Franky.

"Just keep walking, Franky, it'll be off your shoulder soon enough," replied Ted.

"Can we not stop? I can switch with Tam and go to the front."

"You can't stop, Franky, you know that. Keep walking and keep quiet."

"Just suck it up, you big woman," chirped Martin.

"Shut up, you. You're all right, it's on your right shoulder. It's on my left."

"And what?" responded Martin, sensing a chance to wind Franky up.

"There's more strength in your right shoulder."

"How is there? I'm left-handed."

"Well I'm not and it's cutting the fucking shoulder clean off me."

"Keep quiet, you two." Ted interrupted Franky and Martin's squabbling.

The men walked in silence for another couple of minutes.

Franky started again. "Is that undertaker not going to get someone else up for a lift? We've been carrying this for ages."

"We'll finish the lift, Franky. Next stop is the chapel," said Ted.

"Balls! It's fucking miles away. I'll collapse before I get to the chapel. Get that undertaker to grab someone else."

"They've all had lifts, Franky, this is the last one."

"Can they not take another lift?"

"No, they've had theirs."

"Bricklayers… I bet those strangers are bricklayers. Lazy bastards."

"I'm OK," taunted Martin.

"Shut up, you're only using up reserved energy you have through not doing any work when you're at work."

"What are you on about? I work. I always work! Da', tell him, aren't I a good worker?"

"Shut up, the pair of you." Ted was fed up with the bickering.

When they got to the chapel, Franky finally got Jacky's coffin off his back. He started rubbing his shoulder.

"Is that a lead coffin?" he asked Tam.

"No, it's good wood though."

"It'll take ages for the rats to burrow through that coffin. I might get one of those. How much was it?"

"Two thousand pounds," replied Tam.

"Two grand? Fuck that. I'll give that a miss."

At the chapel entrance, Danny the dodger was standing as he is with every funeral.

"Look, Martin. See him, your man, standing over there," Franky pointed to Danny.

"What about him?"

"That's Danny the dodger. He's at every funeral going – a chief pallbearer. When he was thirty, he got a brain tumour. The doctors gave him six months to live."

"What happened? He looks over forty."

"He is! He's forty-three. He goes to every funeral. Since he was given the six months to live, he's buried forty people."

Martin notices Danny take out a piece of paper and jot something down.

"What's that he's writing?" Martin asked Franky.

"That's his tally chart," explained Franky. "Another one ticked off, another one down the hole, before him."

Ted interrupted.

"Martin, dart back to the house and get my glasses. May asked me to do a reading during the mass but I've forgotten them."

"No chance, Ted. The service is about to start. He will never be back in time," replied Tam.

Franky jumped in. "I'll do it."

The three men looked at Franky.

"Are you sure, Franky?" Ted asked. "Would you be able to stand up beside the altar and do a reading?"

"No problem." Franky started to walk towards the chapel doors.

"Wait a minute," said Ted. "Don't you want the reading?"

"Oh, yes, sorry, do you have it there?"

Ted took a piece of paper out of his pocket and handed it to Franky.

"Here, it's a poem. 'He that is down, may fear no fall.' May likes it… it was read out at Jacky Senior's funeral.

Everyone shuffled into the church, taking their seats. Some stood at the back. Franky always stood at the back at funerals. It meant he could nip away for the duration of the mass and come back at the end. No one would know he was away. Not today though. He sat right at the front, rehearsing his routine in his head. It never occurred to him that this might not be the time or place for such, but it was Franky, and in Franky's head, no one else existed.

The priest started the service. It wasn't long before he was calling readers, readings that somehow meant something to Jacky, or his family; readings of love, loss, sorrow, even regret. Some readings are truly beautiful; they can help people in these desperate times of loss.

"I would like to call one of Jacky's closest friends up to say a few words." announced the priest, expecting a psalm or a poem from the reader.

The readings are usually read from the pulpit. On the pulpit was a small microphone. But Franky wasn't going to read from the pulpit; he needed the whole stage to deliver his 'reading'. He grabbed the microphone on the way past but was stopped in his tracks when the cable was only about two feet long. He was forced to do his act from the pulpit. The moment had arrived.

As he stood in the pulpit, he looked down on the congregation – his audience – and he waved to them. "Hello, people. Thanks for coming," he announced sincerely, as if they had come to see him. "Jacky. What can I say about Jacky? I suppose there's one good thing to come out of this… he's finally stopped drinking." He paused for the rapturous laughter. There was none. But Franky wasn't deterred. "You're drunk, people used to say to him. But I can confirm, and his mother's sitting there to testify…" Franky points to May, sitting at the front of the chapel. "… that his name was Jacky, not 'drunk'."

There now seemed to be tumbleweed blowing through the building. Did this idiot not know how serious the Irish took their dead?

He refused to be beaten. "Jacky laughed at me when I told him that I wanted to do stand-up. He's not laughing now."

Even the old Bob Monkhouse joke didn't get a glimmer of a smile from anybody. Some things are so unfunny that they are funny. Jacky doing stand-up at a funeral wasn't one of them. The tumbleweed stopped.

Franky wasn't going to stop. "Drink killed Jacky… I think…"

The microphone was taken off him by The King before he could get any more words out. The King, not wanting any undue stress on May, was gracious in ushering Franky away from the microphone.

"Thank you for the thoughts, Franky. I'd like to say a few words now, if it's OK with you, May."

May nodded her consent.

Franky walked back to his seat meekly. He wasn't put off by the fact that they didn't laugh at any of the jokes. That was just warm up material, he thought. They didn't get a chance to hear the good stuff. He'd have them in stitches next time. That was Franky – delusional to the end.

It was The King's turn to speak. "In the days before he died, I took the opportunity to get to know Jacky again. He knew he was passing. He stared death in the face and showed no fear; he wouldn't buckle. His only worries were his mother and Stacey. Some might say he wasted his life. But his life wasn't a waste to me, Stacey or his mother. Without Jacky, pieces of our lives would be missing. We'll all keep our own individual memories locked away, and for this, Jacky, I will be eternally grateful. Jacky was a victim of the drink culture that surrounded him, and because he was a victim, it makes all of us that knew him or loved him victims. Jacky Johnstone, I salute you."

The King then placed his hand on his heart. Not a salute but a sentiment of love, affection and great sorrow. There was a round of applause in the church, and a few tears. The speech was short but sweet. May was in tears, Stacey was in tears, even Franky got a little emotional, but he had to shake it off. He needed a plan to get out of the church before the collection basket came around.

CHAPTER FOURTEEN
JACKY NEEDS A HAND

After the service and the obligatory visit to the graveyard – where everyone gathers after a funeral, some to make sure the person goes down the hole, some to show their last respects – the boys headed back to May's house. May had left word with Tam to ask the men to call for a drink – only one drink, mind you. She had originally said she wanted no drink at his funeral but she changed her mind to keep to tradition, and she probably didn't want to spend those first few hours alone without Jacky. She didn't like drink but thought the men may not visit if she only offered tea. May had just gone to bed when the first of them arrived. Franky, Ted, Martin and Tam were first there. The talk on the way from the graveyard wasn't of grief, sorrow or loss; it was about Jacky being bald – a secret that the undertaker, Bart the bastard, failed to keep to himself. On arrival at May's house, they congregated in the living room.

"Did you know he was bald and wore a toupee?" Franky asked Tam, seeking confirmation.

"Not until the other day. That undertaker was here. He upset May," replied Tam.

"Why? What did he say to upset her?"

"He wanted to nail the toupee to Jacky's fucking head," Tam explained.

"That's rough," Franky replied. "Could he not have used Gripfill? Or maybe a staple gun to keep his syrup on?"

"What's a syrup?" asked a curious Martin.

"Syrup of fig… a wig. It's cockney rhyming slang."

"Why couldn't you have just said wig?"

"Why don't you just shut up?"

Tam heard movement from upstairs.

"Right, shut up about the wig. It's May… she must be coming downstairs."

May entered the room where the men were sitting. They felt awkward, not knowing what to say.

May broke the silence. "Do any of you want a cup of tea?"

They all declined. They all had a beer.

"Sit down, May, I'll make you a cup," Tam offered.

"No, son, stay where you are. I'll get it myself." May left the living room to make the tea.

There was something on Martin's mind. "Tam, how much was that wreath you bought?"

"I'm not sure, thirty quid I think," replied Tam.

"Thirty pounds? I knew it! Franky, there's no way you paid forty-five pounds for the wreath you got. Tam's was far bigger. The wee shitty one you ended up getting was smaller... it would have been twenty-five max."

"What are you talking about the price of wreaths for? A man's dead and all you can do is talk about the price of a wreath?" said a sanctimonious Franky.

Ted tried to stop the argument in case May overheard.

"Stop it, you two. None of that! Show a wee bit of respect in this girl's home."

Martin wouldn't let it go. "You got fifteen pounds each from us. Where's my change?"

"I bought the wreath for forty-two quid. Do you want your pound change?" replied Franky, denying any wrongdoing.

"There's no way that was forty-two pounds if Tam's was thirty. His is twice as big."

"Would you show some respect? There's a grieving mother in the next room," declared Franky, trying to stop further questioning.

"Me? Show some respect? That's a bit rich. You're the one trying to make money out of a dead man."

"Shut up, the both of you," ordered Ted.

May came back into the room with her tea and sat down. "I don't think I should have risen. I'm so tired, I'm going to go back to bed."

"That's OK, May, we'll go."

"No, Ted, stay and have your drink. I like the sound of people in the house when I lie down. Just stay for a wee while longer."

"If that's what you want, May, we'll stay a bit longer," replied Ted.

May lifted herself off the seat to go back upstairs. Tam bent down to lift her tea to walk her up. Tam followed May upstairs, seeing that she was OK.

As soon as Tam was out of hearing distance, Franky spoke. "Was he wearing a thong there? Just now, when he bent down to pick up May's tea? Did you see it, Martin?" Franky asked.

"I didn't see anything," answered Martin.

"Well, there you go then. I didn't see it either. I bet he was wearing one though. They're not meant to be seen. I reckon it was a black one," said Franky, excitedly.

"Thought you never saw it? How can you tell it was a black one?"

"Because there was a funeral today, stupid. What colour would he be wearing?" answered Franky, sincerely.

"I suppose that makes sense," conceded Martin.

Ted had had enough of the pair of them again.

"What makes sense? None of the pair of you saw anything, so how does it make sense that he was wearing a black thong? Stop all this nonsense... stop getting on like a couple of children. Martin, go to the fridge and get another couple of beers. We'll sit for a while until May settles."

Martin returned with the beers and the three men settled down.

"Sad state of affairs, Jacky dying. You just never know what's around the corner," said Franky, earnestly.

"You're right, Franky, you just never know," replied Ted, glad to be having a serious conversation.

Franky continued. "I think we're all in a queue, Ted."

"What do you mean, Franky?"

"An invisible queue for the grave."

"An invisible queue? What do you mean?" asked Ted, finally listening to something Franky was saying.

"None of us know where we are in the queue. We just know we're in it. We don't know how far up the line we are, or how far back, we can't see the end of it, nor the start of it. We wait alone, waiting... waiting... waiting... never knowing when we'll reach the front. Are you into all this God nonsense, Ted?"

"Not really, Franky. At my age, it would be nice to know there was something there when we check out though."

"So, you don't go to mass anymore?"

"I do, Franky. I look on it as a wee insurance policy."

"What do you mean?"

"If someone pays an insurance policy, they pay a couple of pounds a week. If something happens to you, they pay out. I go to mass a couple of hours a week, just in case. If there's a God, I'll get paid. If not, it's only a couple of hours a week, no big deal."

"I'm not sure it works that way, Ted. I think you need to truly believe."

"I live a good life, Franky. I harm nobody and I do my best for people. If that doesn't afford me a place in any afterlife, then I simply don't want to be there. What kind of place would it be? It would be full of people I try to avoid here, so why would I want to spend an eternity with them?"

"But hell's going to be full of people you avoid on Earth, too, Ted. You're going to lose either way."

"Then, Franky, will it really be so bad if there's nothing?"

Martin, listening intently to the conversation, had something to add. "Life is just a slither of light in-between two eternities of darkness."

"That's a bit profound... did you think of that, yourself?" asked Franky.

"No, I heard someone say it on 'Father Ted' the other night."

Franky was irritated again. "You see what I mean, Ted? This is where the young ones get their education these days. Silly TV shows, Facebook and corner conversations. The world's doomed."

The boys were interrupted by a knock on the door. Stacey popped her head in. "How's May keeping, Ted? Is she OK?"

"She's not bad, love. Tam took her upstairs to get her to sleep."

"Do you want a wee drink, love?" asked Ted.

"I'll just have one. Is May OK with us having a wee drink here?"

"She's OK. She insisted. What do you want?"

"I think she has a wee bottle of Pimm's in the cupboard. I'll have a Pimm's with lemonade and ice, if that's OK?"

"No problem, Stacey. You heard the girl, Martin, go and get her a drink, will you?"

Ted wasn't asking Martin to get her a drink; he was telling him. Martin obliged and went off to the kitchen to fix the drink.

Stacey sat down. "It's not right, Ted. A mother having to bury her child… it's just not natural," said Stacey, not knowing what to say.

"It would be an awful thing for anyone to have to do," answered Ted.

Franky didn't totally agree with this train of thought and felt the need to say so. "I don't know about that. I want to live as long as I can and, if it means burying my children, so be it."

Stacey was taken aback somewhat by this statement. "You don't mean that, Franky, that's a terrible thing to say."

Franky, realising the disgust on Stacey's face at this comment, tried to backtrack. "I didn't mean it like that. I meant, I want to live as long as I can to look after them."

"So, you want to be alive to look after them, but don't mind burying them at the same time?" asked Stacey, a little angry.

"Stop mincing my words. Of course, I would mind if they die. I just want to be around in their hour of need."

Martin returned from the kitchen and handed Stacey her drink. He was listening to the conversation from the kitchen and decided to wind Franky up. "What did you say there, Franky? You want all your children to die first?"

"I didn't say I wanted my children to die first. I said I wanted to be around to look after them."

"You're trying to dig yourself out of a hole now," taunted Martin.

"I'm not trying to dig myself out of a hole. And another thing, why, in emergency situations, do women and children get preference? In a hostage situation, women and children go first. A ship going down, women and children go first. Plane crash, women and children rescued first. It doesn't seem fair at all."

"They let the women and children go first because they are the most vulnerable," answered Ted.

"So what if they're more vulnerable? Women, children, then the disabled, then men… or do the animals get saved before men? It's a joke. I don't care who's the most vulnerable. If that ship's going down, I'll be on the lifeboat as fast as I can. Before the women, before the children, before the disabled and before the animals."

"You can't do that, Franky. You're an able-bodied man. You have to let them on before you," pleaded Stacey.

"No fucking way are the disabled getting on that lifeboat before me! I'll just limp over to it and jump in. Why not? Everybody will be doing it."

Stacey looked down at her glass and noticed that Martin didn't put any ice in her drink. "Was there no ice, Martin?"

"Sorry, Stacey, I didn't know you wanted any… give me your glass, I'll go and get you some."

Martin took Stacey's glass and returned once again to the kitchen to get her ice. But he came back in hysterical laughter, holding a Tupperware box. He threw the box on Franky's lap. "Here, Franky… do you think that'll come in *handy*?"

Franky looked down at the contents of the container and immediately threw it to the ground.

"What the *fuck* is that?"

"What *is* that?" asked Stacey, looking at it with disgust but not knowing what she was looking at.

"What is it?" asked Ted.

"It's a hand! May has a hand in her freezer," answered Martin, still laughing.

Ted picked up the box and examined it further. "Sweet Jesus, so it is… it is a hand. Where did you get this?"

"It was in the freezer. I found it when I was looking for the ice."

"Put it back where you found it," ordered Ted.

"Put it back where?" interrupted Franky. "In-between the fish fingers and the bag of frozen peas?"

"Shut up, Franky. Put it back where you found it, Martin. It's none of our business."

"Jesus, Ted, do you think she's a serial killer? She may have spiked our drinks! That's why she wanted us to come back."

"I better put this back in the freezer. If it defrosts, it'll stink the place out," declared a concerned Martin.

"Why are you laughing about it, anyway?" Franky asked Martin. "You walked in like it was a frozen salmon with a squint. It's a severed hand! Don't you know that severed body parts aren't the least bit funny? Did they not teach you that at the corner? Or on Facebook?"

"How's May having a hand in her freezer not funny? Of course it's funny."

"It's *not* funny. Anyway, the question is, how did it get there?" asked Franky.

"Maybe that old undertaker put it there… he looked a right evil bastard," replied Martin.

"Watch your language, Martin."

"Sorry, da'."

"Don't be silly, Martin. Why would that undertaker put an arm in the freezer?" Franky asked Martin.

"Big Tam said he was arrested for arm robbery before."

"*Armed* robbery, you mean."

"No, *arm* robbery… he was stealing arms from the morgue."

"He was stealing arms from the morgue? Why would he do that?"

"I don't know, maybe he was trying to gather up his own *army*," Martin thought this was hilarious. Taunting Franky was always fun; funnier though when you were taunting him about a severed hand.

"Very funny," said Franky.

Ted had had enough, it was time to get serious. "Stop saying it was an arm just to make up jokes about it. It's a hand. Right, what we saw here today has never to be spoken of again. Understood?"

"We can't say anything? There's a hand in that freezer, Ted, and we don't know who owns it. It could be one of ours for all we know."

Everyone looked down at their hands to make sure their own two were attached to their arms.

"I've got mine," said Martin.

"So do I," said Stacey.

"I don't mean *literally* one of ours. I meant it could be off someone we know," retorted Franky

"Well, the last I looked, all my family and friends had their two hands. Therefore, I'm declaring this none of my business. If all your family and friends have both hands, I suggest you do the same." Ted knew the seriousness of what they were dealing with.

"I don't know anybody missing a hand. I know someone missing a few toes though," quipped Martin.

"Who? Are you talking about Paddy? Who dropped a concrete block on his toes? What's that got to do with anything?" asked Franky.

"I'm only saying."

"I'll tell you what… go and see if Paddy's toes are in May's freezer. If they are, we'll throw them back round to him."

"You never know," whimpered Martin.

"You never know, what? The toes were brought to the hospital with him that day. They tried to sew them back on. Do you think May called round that night… 'Here, doctor, I heard you couldn't sew Paddy's toes back on… any chance of giving them to me, so I can stick them in my freezer?'"

"Don't be so smart, Franky. She had a hand in her freezer. I dare say she's capable of anything."

"Listen, Martin. Even if she was capable of it, do you think the people in the hospital are just going to hand over Paddy's toes? 'No problem, May, here's Paddy's toes. There was a motorbike accident earlier so call back because we might have an ear, an ankle and a pair of balls for you, if the operation isn't successful…'"

Tam returned to the living room from upstairs. He was unaware of what was happening, but they soon enlightened him.

"What the fuck is a hand doing in May's freezer, Tam?" asked Franky.

"A what?"

"A hand, Tam. A severed human hand. Did you know it was there?"

Everyone looked at Tam. Tam, in return, scanned the room, looking them all in the face. If it was his own house, he would throw them out, there and then, but it wasn't his home, it was May's. He knew they couldn't un-see what they had seen, so he had some explaining to do.

"Yes, I did know it was there." He looked at Martin. "I bet it was you who found it, acting the bollocks, snooping about in other people's freezers."

Ted jumped to his son's defence. "He wasn't *acting the bollocks*, Tam. He went to get ice. If I had have known there were body parts stored there, I wouldn't have sent him. In fact, I wouldn't even be in this house. How did you know it was there?"

"I put it there, Ted."

"Right, that's OK. We don't want to know why you put it there, when you put it there, or who owns it. As far as we're concerned, we never set eyes on it."

Martin, not listening to his father, asked the question on everyone's mind: "Whose hand is it, Tam?"

Tam gave Martin a dirty look. Without saying anything, he walked right past everyone into the kitchen. When he went out of view, Franky lifted a smoothing iron and hid it behind his back.

"What are you going to do with that?" asked Stacey.

"He knows. We know. Do you think that big psycho's going to let us out of here alive?" replied Franky.

"And what are you going to do with that? Smooth him to death?" said Martin, laughing.

Tam returned drinking a bottle of beer. He looked around the room at the people in front of him, and spoke. "May owns the hand."

Franky looked puzzled. "I wasn't paying much attention, but the last time May was in here, I could have sworn she had two hands. I think a one-handed old lady is something I would have noticed."

Martin butts in. "I never noticed how many hands she had."

"She has *two* hands," confirms Ted. "Tam, you don't need to explain."

"I do, Ted. I do need to explain. I don't want any rumours going about. Next thing you know, May and I will be the new Fred and Rose West, for fuck's sake."

"There'll be no rumours, Tam. I'll make sure of that."

"I know how they talk, Ted. There was a rumour going around last week that I wear women's underwear." Tam gave Martin a dirty look. Martin and Franky looked at each other, wanting to laugh, but too frightened to do so.

Tam continued. "The hand belonged to Jacky. May asked me to cut it off, so she could keep a part of him. I cut it off an hour before they closed the coffin. It was *Jacky's* hand. Now it's May's."

"You cut it off? You cut it off before they closed the coffin? Jesus Christ, what with nailing his head and cutting off his hand, a small renovation would have less work done on it."

"She was heartbroken, devastated. She wanted to keep part of her son with her. I tried to talk her out of it, but she wouldn't listen."

"What did you cut it off with?"

"An angle grinder."

"Holy fuck, an angle grinder? Why didn't you use a hacksaw?"

"It had to be quick and clean."

Stacey was feeling sick to the stomach at the thoughts of this happening to Jacky.

"How could you do that? You fucking animal!"

"I'm sorry, Stacey. I had to. May wouldn't take no for an answer."

"What happens now, Tam?" asked Franky. "You just can't keep a hand in a freezer... not now we all know about it."

"Why not?" replied Tam.

Ted seemed to be the only one who grasped the absurdity of the situation. He tried to inject some sense into the conversation.

"It's not right, Tam. When we leave, she'll probably take it to bed with her or something... sit with it on her lap... it's just not right."

"She'll probably make two cups of tea every night and wrap the hand around one of them," joked Martin, who hadn't grasped the seriousness of the situation.

"And so what if she does? She'll be doing no harm."

"Tam, it'll defrost, decompose and go putrid," explained Ted, the voice of reason.

"I told her all of this. She said she wouldn't take it out of the freezer."

Franky sat in silence for a change. He had his thinking cap on. "When did you cut it off?"

"An hour before the coffin closed."

"Didn't anyone notice?"

"No, everyone had already paid their respects. Anyway, I put his Man United top over it to cover it."

"This year's Man United top?" inquired Franky.

"*Yes*, Franky, this year's top. The one he liked. I put it in the coffin so nobody would be any the wiser."

"Why couldn't you have used a towel or something?"

"How could I have used a towel? Who gets buried in a towel?"

"Indians," Martin chirped in.

"What?" asked Tam.

"Indians get buried in towels," Martin reaffirmed.

Franky was getting irritated again. "Turbans they're called. Turbans. Don't they teach you that on Facebook?"

Franky wasn't finished with questioning Tam. The thoughts of a new football top that fitted him getting buried with Jacky was driving him to despair.

"Why didn't you put that T-shirt over his hands?" Franky pointed to the shirt Tam was wearing. "That's Jacky's, too, isn't it?"

"My own shirt was all sweaty… it's an old one. Why do you give a fuck anyway?"

"I could have had that Man United top… it's just a waste burying it."

Stacey was near breaking point. "Stop it! Stop it. Stop arguing over his clothes like a pair of fucking scavengers."

Martin was starting to smell a rat with Tam's story. "When did you cut it off again?"

"Earlier," answered Tam.

"Sure. I was here the whole time, before the undertaker came to take him away."

"I did it when I asked you all to leave so that I could close the coffin."

"That's impossible. There was no electric. You couldn't have used an angle grinder."

"There was electric."

"No, there wasn't. May sent me round to get money on her electric card when you told everybody to leave the room. I was just leaving for the shop."

"Who the fuck do you think you are? Colombo? I used a hacksaw."

"You said an angle grinder."

"I forgot."

Franky interrupted. "Where's the blood? The bits of skin? The pieces of bone?"

Tam had nothing more to say as the room fell to silence. Martin returned once more to the kitchen.

Franky wouldn't let up about the football top. "I can't believe you buried him in that good football top. United's playing Chelsea next week. It would have come in handy."

Franky's obsession with the football top is now starting to anger Tam. "Shut the fuck up about the football top, will you? If you don't shut up about it, then I will fuck you up."

Before any more words were exchanged, Martin returned from the kitchen. He had taken the hand out of the freezer again. He had removed it from the container.

Stacey was disgusted. "Martin, put that away. Don't be so gross."

"Put it away? What for? It's wood..." Martin tapped the hand on the table. "It's as wooden as Franky's jokes."

Martin gave the hand to his father, who examined it. "It *is* wood," Ted confirmed.

It was passed around so everyone could see and feel for themselves that it was, in fact, a wooden hand. They all had a turn checking it out. While they were scrutinising it, they failed to notice May. She was up out of bed and silently standing at the back of the room. She watched as they passed the mannequin's hand around. Tam spotted her first. He turned very sheepish all of a sudden, as May spoke directly to him.

"So, you couldn't do it, Tam? He's gone forever now. All of him is gone. You promised me."

"I couldn't, May. It just wasn't right."

"How long did you think that mannequin's hand was going to fool me? You could have done it, but you didn't. You made me a promise, and broke it."

Ted had heard enough of this madness. "For fuck's sake, May, enough of this nonsense. We've been friends as long as I can remember. I'm telling you now that this is not right. It's not normal behaviour. You have your memories. That's all we get... memories. Savour them, cherish them, dwell on them, do whatever you have to do with them because it's *all* we get. Nothing else."

May stared at Ted. She knew he was right, but the stomach-churning thoughts of her boy being gone forever had dampened her senses.

Stacey saw a way out. "He was a Catholic anyway, May."

May looked at Stacey for an explanation to her comment.

Stacey continued. "May, he has to be buried whole. His whole body intact, or he'll not get into heaven, if there is a heaven."

May stared at Stacey for a few seconds, then she turned to Ted. "Is that right, Ted?"

"You know I'm not a believer, May, but she is right... the Catholic Church says the body has to be whole to enter The Kingdom of Heaven. Better not taking any chances."

May stood silent. She was drained. She looked around the room at everyone. They looked back.

She addressed Tam. "Well, it's just as well you didn't go through with it then, Tam, son. I'm going up for another wee lie down. You can see yourselves out."

And just like that, May came to her senses. It's as if she needed something to grab onto. She knew she was wrong in what she wanted to do, but she needed proof that it was wrong. She grabbed onto the Catholic Church doctrine that a body must be buried whole for your soul to go to heaven. At least she came to her senses.

As May went to walk out of the room, back to bed, Tam had something for her. "Here, May. I took this off Jacky, just before the coffin was closed. There's a wee bit of tape still on it, where they taped it to Jacky's head." Tam handed May the toupee.

"Oh, thank you, son. At least I have something," said May, taking the toupee off Tam.

May said her goodbyes and went up to bed. She consoled herself in the fact that it wasn't Jacky's own hair, so it wouldn't stop him getting into heaven.

"Good thinking, Tam, taking that off his head before the coffin closed. At least it's something for her," said Martin.

"That wasn't Jacky's," Tam admitted. "I got it off the same dummy I got the hand from..."

"What were you doing with it in your pocket?"

"Never you mind."

"Why didn't you just slip Jacky's actual toupee off for her?"

"Because it was nailed to his fucking head."

CHAPTER FIFTEEN
THE END GAME

A few hours after her guests had left, May awoke to an empty house. She lay in bed thinking about the funeral. It was a good turnout, she thought. He was well-liked, my Jacky. A good old soul. She thought about all the well-wishers.

'He's in a better place now.'

'God only takes the best.'

But the one she disliked the most: 'His suffering's over.' What did they mean by this? 'His suffering's over'? What suffering? Jacky didn't suffer. He loved life. He had the life of luxury, sitting drinking his cider, no worries, no responsibilities, never working, getting up when he wanted, getting his dinner handed to him. She did wonder whether he was in a better place now. Was she being selfish, wanting him here? Here, where she could still visit him? Her mind was numb. She would get through this though. She would survive. Because if there was anything that May was, it was exactly that: a survivor. She couldn't sleep any more that evening, the evening of the funeral. She got out of bed, washed her face and went downstairs. No sooner had she put the kettle on, the door knocked. It was The King.

Although Stacey didn't live with Jacky, the loneliness hit her like a ton of bricks when she entered her house on the evening of Jacky's funeral. The loneliness she felt was indescribable. The pain was indescribable. She would never set eyes on him again. This reality had set in. Mixed with the guilt, the sorrow and the fear, it was the worst night of her life and she knew it wouldn't get much better in the days, weeks, months, or even years ahead. At the graveyard, as the dirt started falling on Jacky's coffin, she had a very strange emotion. She would never see the love of her life again, but that dirt was going to cover up her crime. She'd be safe. Off the hook. Was this emotion relief? Mixed with sorrow? She cried, of course, as she had done every night from the moment he died. She cried herself to sleep again the night of his funeral. About an hour into sleep, she was woken by her phone. It was a text message. Who would be texting her? Rubbing her eyes, she looked at the name that flashed up on her phone. May. May was asking her to go around to her house. Poor May, Stacey thought. She must be lonely. Stacey herself could use some company. She readied herself, put on a little make-up, and headed around to May's house.

****

Franky sat watching the TV that evening, the evening of the funeral. He knew there was no police investigation into Jacky's death, so he was safe. There was one thing that annoyed him though: that football top. He continually cursed Tam for wasting it. May said Jacky would have old working coats. She brought round the boots. Franky's name was on that top. That Tam's a wanker, he thought. Then he had another thought. If Tam didn't really cut off Jacky's hand, why would he need to put that football top in the coffin? That big bastard, he thought. Tam's going to keep that top for himself. The other T-shirt fitted him, so the football top would fit him. You couldn't be up to that big fucker. He'll investigate further, when he sees Tam in work the next day.

His thoughts now turned to the big, fancy coffin that Jacky got buried in. The big one that went down the hole to be buried forever. Did May have money? Did Jacky have money? It must be May. It's May who has the money. It couldn't be Jacky; that fucker was always skint. If Jacky had any money, he would have bought that blow the night he died. That blow? He still had that blow. Nearly a hundred pounds' worth. He was going to bring it to the bar that day, see if he could even get fifty quid for it.

He did his usual stunt. When Ted, Martin and himself left May's house, he said he would follow them to the pub, but he forgot he left his heating on. He would do this so he wouldn't have to buy the first round. He would take a bottle of beer from the house while pretending to put his heating on. This enabled him not to drink too fast when he eventually got to the bar, therefore not being under any pressure to buy the second round. He meant to lift the weed then, but forgot. He was just about to have another look at Jacky's boots when he got a text. It was May. What does she want? She knows where he lives. Maybe she had pulled out those old working coats? Maybe that big fucker Tam never took the top. Was she keeping it for him? No matter, there was bound to be something in it for him. The new TV? No, surely she couldn't be giving that away so soon. No matter. He'd soon see. Franky bolted around to May's.

****

Tam's only thoughts, when the dirt went down on Jacky earlier that day, were for May. Tam never thought that he ended Jacky's life; he just brought forward the inevitable. Jacky was on his way out, he told himself, it would be sooner rather than later. The undertaker approached Tam for payment as he left the graveyard. He never mentioned the amount, for fear of having another fifty pounds taken off. They agreed Tam would call the following week and settle the bill.

He was now at home after the shenanigans at May's house earlier. He put on his black lacy underwear and was about to settle down for a drink. He hadn't worn the lacy underwear earlier at the funeral, as a mark of respect for May. The first time he hadn't worn them in years. But then he got a text message. It was May. She wanted to see him. Unusual, he thought. She never texts. He'd best go around to her house; she'll need someone to talk to. Tam put on his coat and sauntered on round to May's.

****

Stacey tapped lightly, then opened the back door of May's house. She walked on in. She knew May was expecting her.

She called for May as she walked through the kitchen. "May, are you home?"

"I'm in the living room." May beckoned her in.

As Stacey entered the living room, her heart dropped at what she saw. The King was sitting on the settee with May. They had a deadly serious look about them both. Stacey felt like being sick. She knew The King knew something about what had happened because of what he had said in the bar the night before.

May asked Stacey to sit down.

Stacey sat down on the chair facing May and The King. She was dreading what she was about to hear.

"Why didn't you tell me, Stacey?" May asked, as earnest as Stacey had ever heard her speak.

"Tell you what, May?"

"That you were the last one to see my Jacky alive."

"Me? But…"

"Did you phone an ambulance for him, Stacey?"

"May I…"

"Did you kill him, Stacey? Did you kill the man you love? My son?"

Stacey was never too good at lying and no good at lying under this kind of pressure. She started sobbing. "He was already dead, May. There was nothing I or anyone else could have done. He took those pills…"

"What pills?"

"Those Viagra tablets."

"What are Viagra tablets?" May asked.

"It's to get a man an erection," said Stacey, quietly, still sobbing.

"Why would you let him take those on top of his own medication? Surcly you know how dangerous that is?"

"I don't know, May. I don't know why I let him take them. I don't know what medication he was on."

"Where did he get them?"

On hearing this, Stacey quickly twigged that they didn't know the full story. They didn't know that *she* had brought them to Jacky's house that evening. "I don't know, May. He phoned me to come around. He had already taken them."

"Why didn't you phone an ambulance?"

"The shame. I didn't want everyone talking about me again."

"You let my son *die* to save yourself a little embarrassment?"

"I couldn't save him," sobbed Stacey, rubbing her eyes with a handkerchief.

The King sat silent. He was staring at Stacey, without a hint of emotion. He decided to speak. "If you had nothing to do with him taking ill, and you didn't know how to handle it when he did, why didn't you phone an ambulance?"

"I don't know. I just panicked."

The room fell silent. Stacey didn't know how to defend the fact that she didn't phone an ambulance for him. May turned her face away from Stacey. Stacey knew it was time to leave. She wasn't fully rumbled, but as good as. She never phoned that ambulance. As she left, she realised that not phoning for the ambulance was as good as killing him.

It took around ten seconds for Stacey to rise from the chair and walk to the door. It seemed like a lifetime. Before she left, she looked back at May, as if to get some reassurance. But there was none. May didn't even look at her leaving. She couldn't. As Stacey walked to the door, she felt more than ever the very thing that stopped her phoning the ambulance: shame.

****

Franky came to the door about twenty minutes later. He called for May at the back door and was beckoned into the living room. The King and May were sitting in the same place. Franky automatically sat where Stacey had sat. He wasn't that concerned about seeing The King sitting there. After all, Jacky was dead and buried. He would deny everything. What does this clown with his voodoo shit know? Fuck all, he thought.

"Why did you give Jacky drugs on the night he died, Franky?" May asked him, in a whisper.

"What are you talking about, May? I'm a working man, not a drug dealer. I never gave him any drugs."

"My son's gone, Franky. Why didn't you help him?"

"I don't know what you're talking about, May."

The King was staring at Franky. He decided to speak. "You gave him heroin, then you left him to die."

Franky was absolutely shocked at this statement. Heroin? What the fuck was he talking about?

The King continued. "You gave him heroin. You left him to die. Her son. *My* friend. Why did you do that?"

Franky was now afraid. Heroin? Fucking heroin? There was no way he could prove that it wasn't heroin now Jacky was buried.

He decided to put the record straight. "I brought him a wee bit of grass, for fuck's sake. A wee bit of grass. To help him with the pain. I'm not Pablo fucking Escobar."

"You brought my son drugs? How could you?"

"He asked me to, May. He was in pain. I told him not to take drugs, but he went on and on. I felt sorry for him, what with the chest pains and the liver and that."

"You left him to die. You didn't phone an ambulance."

"He was dead when I left. What good would an ambulance have done? That ambulance may have been needed in an emergency somewhere else. Did you ever think of that?"

There was nothing else to say to Franky. His presence in the house was starting to annoy The King and May. The King stared daggers at him.

Franky knew it was time to leave. Franky walked to the back door in which he had entered. As he opened it, he got a tap on his shoulder. It was The King.

"I think May deserves a nice, big headstone for Jacky, don't you, Franky?"

"Of course she does, but if you're looking me to chip in, I've only got twenties on me."

"You're paying for it."

"What? Will I fuck! They're about two grand."

"Not the one she likes. It's three thousand. That one will do nicely. I'll let you know the inscription."

"Fuck off…"

"May would never phone the police. She's old school. But I would. You would be done for selling drugs – a big fine, solicitors, then jail."

"You can prove nothing."

"If I ring the police now, they'll be searching your house before you get there, even if you run."

"That's shite. How do you know I won't get there first?"

"I know because I am The King."

"And what if I say I'll pay, renege, then dump the grass?"

"Then when I phone the police, I'll make sure there are drugs there… only it *will* be heroin."

"You can't do that."

"I can because I am The King."

Franky looked into The King's eyes. He knew he couldn't win this one. Him and his voodoo shit, he's capable of anything.

"OK, you win, I'll pay for the headstone," Franky said.

Franky left May's house disgusted with himself. He shouldn't have gone to Jacky's that night. Going to Jacky's meant he lost two friends in Jacky and May. That didn't concern him much though. Going to Jacky's that night had cost him much, much more: three grand.

****

Around thirty minutes later, Tam arrived. He didn't shout or knock. He walked straight into the living room. The King and May were still on the settee.

"You OK, May? Were you looking for me?" Tam asked a solemn-faced May.

The King was the first to speak to him. "You were with Jacky the night he died. You left him to die. Why?"

Tam looked at The King, then looked at May. May couldn't bear to look at him.

"Who the fuck are you? Shaft?" Tam said.

"Were you with him?" May whispered.

Tam hated lying to May. He lied about the hand, but that was for her own good. He wasn't going to start lying to her now. "I was, May. I hit him. I hit him and left him. I don't know if he was dead. He might have been. I left in a rage."

"Why, Tam? Why did you hit him?"

There was no way Tam was telling May the spew that came out of her son's mouth that night. He would die first. He decided, for the second time that day, to do something he had never done before: to lie to her. "I told him he wasn't fit to be your son. We got into a fight… he took it bad. He warned me not to talk about his mother in that tone of voice. He said his mother meant the world to him. He hit me. I hit him back… harder. I went into that zone, I couldn't help myself."

May's face lit up. "Did he really say that? Did he really say that, Tam?"

"As sure as I'm standing here, May. He wouldn't let me say a word about you."

The King, of course, knew that this was a nonsense. He admired the way Tam said it though, giving May a little pleasure in all her misery.

"Why didn't you phone an ambulance, son?"

"I did, May. I phoned it as soon as I got home. Too little, too late. I'm sorry. Can you forgive me, May?"

May looked at Tam. She looked right into his eyes. "I forgive you, Tam."

Tam was relieved, for a split second he thought he had gotten away with it. Then May spoke again. "I don't ever want to see you around here again. I'll be fine without you calling.

"But, May…" He didn't finish what he was going to say. May turned her head. He was going to plead a case for himself, but there was none. He decided not to try. He turned and walked out the door. He walked down the street towards home. That was the evening Tam lost the most precious thing he had in the world: May.

****

Of course, The King and May knew that neither one of the three had killed Jacky. The cause of death was liver failure, due to cirrhosis. Any one of the three incidents could have brought it on, but then again, none of the incidents may have brought it on. It was more than likely a coincidence that Jacky had died that night.

The King, through Jacky's incoherent chatter as he was wheeled down the path and into the ambulance that night, could get a little piece of the picture. The fact that none of them mentioned to anybody else that they were on the scene that night had also caused him to smell a rat. He knew rightly that none of these three people had killed him, because he was there and Jacky was alive long after they had gone. But the three of them didn't know that. It was the way these people left Jacky to die that upset The King the most.

The King had spent time with May the day after Jacky's death. During their conversations, The King learned how much these people meant to her. He couldn't understand how they could let her down in her hour of need. The King got May to summon them that night so that he could shame them. This wasn't why May wanted to see them though. She wanted to know about her son's last day on Earth. May wasn't one for revenge or vengeance. Although the three may not have got their comeuppance for leaving a friend to die, they lost something greater: an unconditional friend. A friend who would travel to the end of the world for her friends and not ask a question.

May would be able to spend the rest of her years with her head held high. She had nothing, but she had everything. Her decency would always shine, and she was ashamed of nothing.

THE END

Printed in Great Britain
by Amazon